Waltzing Cowboys

SARAH COLLINS
HONENBERGER

Cedar Creek Publishing
Virginia, USA

Cover image "Boots" by E.E. McNeel
www.angleofreposephotography.com

Author photo by Mary Davis

Cedar Creek Publishing
Bremo Bluff, Virginia
www.cedarcreekauthors.com

Printed in the United States of America

Library of Congress Control Number 2008932012

ISBN 978-0-9790205-6-8

Waltzing Cowboys

White Lies
A Tale of Babies, Vaccines, and Deception
ISBN 978-0-9790205-1-3

". . . a fine new novelist . . . Honenberger is a gifted storyteller, a master of nuance who knows how to move you deeply; how to lift your heart; how to grab your attention and hold it."
— Copley News Service

"A lesson in how the quietest fiction can often be the most powerful."
— *Meridian* Editor, Stephen Boykewich

"I convinced myself that no one would really buy a book based on its opening chapter. I was wrong. I read Sarah Collins Honenberger's first chapter on her web site, http://www.readwhitelies.com/, and promptly went out and bought the book. I was excited, angry, sad, concerned, disturbed, because that's what the characters deserved, because the author had made me care. If you're looking for a really good read, with two fascinating, flawed, wise and wonderful lead characters . . . this book fulfilled its promise."
— Sheila Deeth, Gather.com reviewer

"Honenberger's *White Lies* is a compelling account of tragedy, but it is also a compelling portrayal of heroism and how complicated and difficult it is to right a wrong. Here is a courtroom drama of the highest order, where the human scale of justice and suffering is beautifully portrayed. *White Lies* is a wonderfully sympathetic and knowing portrait of a sorrowing mother and the attorney who came to her aid."
— Carrie Brown, Author
The Hatbox Baby, Confinement,
Rose's Garden, and *The House at Belle Isle*

"*White Lies* is startlingly well written. That Honenberger succeeds in making this fast-paced intrigue a truly memorable novel places her in the upper echelon of new writers. We will be hearing more from Sarah Collins Honenberger."
— Grady Harp, Top Five Amazon Reviewer

Dedicated to Walt Whitman,
a fellow New Englander, who understood
the magic of unexplored places and far horizons

Waltzing Cowboys

Chapter One

*R*hue stared at the edge of the freshly ditched ground. He thought maybe he'd died too, the colors all washed out in the bright noon light, and the silence so long and heavy it dragged his feet into a dirge of dust and dread. How close he felt to death. The longer he stared, the more comfortable it looked, that level dry earth with indentations for his hunched shoulders and his weary hips. Maybe he should leave Montana, go somewhere new, anywhere, not wait for death or the nursing home, not wait as if he'd conceded there was no future.

Forcing himself to leave Vince's grave, he walked with more energy than he felt to the truck. It coughed, but started. Probably time for a new battery. He tried to remember when he'd bought the last one. Where the cemetery's rutted grass pathway ended, he turned onto the pavement and let the truck roll downhill. Without thinking about where he was headed, he made a left at the state road and wound down the valley from the county cemetery, a curling tail of blue-black smoke trailing in his wake.

The truck needed more than a battery. Despite the cracked rearview mirror, he could see the sun hovering on the ridge. It quivered red and orange, as anxious to be done with this sorry day as he was.

Rather than turning in at the ranch entrance, he let the truck drift to a stop in the road and surveyed the barnyard. He didn't want to run into the absentee owner. Their last argument lingered like rotting corn husks in a hog's slop bucket.

"You're making the boys nervous," the faceless Los Angeles businessman had said with the blare of car horns in the background.

"You hired them."

"They have a job to do. I've got twenty-five horses due in Kalispell on the 16th. They don't have time to be distracted."

"You want those horses trained or just scared to death?"

"Listen, old man. I appreciate you were the expert." Ringing phones and the sound of voice over voice sliced across their conversation like sirens. "Once upon a time. But now it's time to move on. The boys would do fine if you weren't watching over their shoulders every day, throwing out critiques like a two-bit county fair judge."

"You barring me from the ranch?" The pressure was building in his chest.

"I didn't say that. Everyone's trying to be respectful. Just quit with the opinions. Let 'em do their job."

Rhue had wanted to say that was wishful thinking, but it wasn't worth risking an outright no trespass warning. He understood the pressure to produce quarter horses that could perform. He'd done it for decades. It wasn't that this new breed of part-time cowboy couldn't learn how. They just didn't seem to be invested in it like he and Vince and Marian had been. It was hard to watch.

The truck idled at the gate while he considered whether to risk going up to the corral. His alternative, the empty apartment, wasn't appealing, though. Only one other truck was parked by the barn. Maybe they'd already quit for the day.

Vince's funeral had spoiled more than the afternoon. It seemed so long ago that he'd lifted the loose board that was Vince's makeshift gate and whistled for his best friend. And now they'd buried him. A parade of old men, barely able to lift the coffin, had walked with Vince that one last time.

Forty years earlier when they'd met, Vince had been young and wild, and so had he, even at thirty-nine. Confused and angry, he'd left New York City and a pregnant wife without understanding why. He only knew he had to escape. After ten years in an office, with schedules and expectations, not only from Adriana but also from his parents, colleagues, clients, he'd been relieved to find a place where he could let go of the worry and burden of people depending on his happiness for their own.

He had regrets, and his boy was one of them, but staying would've soured them all. In this world he was a traveler, not meant for staking out a place and guarding it. Who knew what he'd be in the next world?

He and Vince, they'd covered some trails between them. And Marian, too. She'd been their straight man. Locked in her head were the mountain passes and the springs and the wildcat havens, all etched out so they knew almost the day they met how much they needed her. But if they hadn't dared her, she might not have taken them to those places where her Indian ancestors hunted. During all their years of reining in canyon pintos and sleeping by campfires, she had more than kept up, not to compete with the two guys as much as that she didn't suffer fools.

But on his last couple of visits to the nursing home, Marian—her hands twisted in the cord of her bathrobe, the muscles gone slack with idleness—didn't recognize him. All their convoluted explorations of ideas and hopes between saddle and creek bed were locked behind that expressionless face. She didn't remember.

With Vince gone and Marian rocking away in a world of her own, suddenly Rhue felt his age. He was old, older than he'd ever expected to be. He had dark stains on the backs of his hands and a crooked place in his spine. His hair had turned; bleach blond to earthy gray. And then, like the victims of trauma, before he even realized it, it turned white as the new lambs he remembered from childhood summers seventy-odd years ago. It was as if he awoke one morning to a revelation that screamed, "You're done here. Get gone." Time, without asking or warning, had announced its own abdication. Of all people, he had no right to claim surprise.

Still, he wasn't sure which was worse. The strange familiarity of the gravesite had been comforting, but Marian, sitting in the dark overheated room, humming odd phrases and mimicking voices in the hall, made him fume, white hot angry but helpless, the way a steer gets when his foreleg folds and he knows he's down. Rhue didn't go often to see her. The Marian he knew was flying bareback across the range.

The horses, though, were the same. Their heads still rose at his step. It fascinated him how clear their eyes were and the way their nostrils flared in anticipation. Most days before the sun came up he went to watch them in the field. He sat on the open tailgate until the ranch hands ambled up to the barn. Billows of dust, ghostly soldiers, lagged behind them. Like company, the warmth from the truck's temperamental heater crept out and sat beside him. Sometimes he stayed until after sunset, until after the men went in to eat supper at the long warped table where he used to sit. From the corral he could smell the beans. He could taste them.

He pushed the accelerator, let the truck swing wide and bump up the dirt drive. Parking alone on the near side of the barn, he figured if he walked around, whoever it was might not even know he was here. Before he left the truck, he stripped off his jacket and the tie borrowed from his neighbor, the Laundromat operator, a talkative little Chinese man who bowed and smiled as if Rhue were his best client.

"Keep, keep," he'd said as he tugged it out of the lost and found bag at the Laundromat. Once he heard it was for Vince's funeral, he handed it over with ceremony as if it were Rhue's birthday.

"Thanks," Rhue said, "but not much call for me wearing a tie. I'll drop it off here when the funeral's over."

"Never know. Alway be prepared if you keep. Tie not take much room."

"Thanks, anyway." He'd wondered how the fellow knew he was concerned about taking up space with things.

Sitting on the lip of the water trough, Rhue made a quick head count in the corral. Under the fence posts where the grass grew untrimmed, the horses were grazing hungrily as if it were their first meal of the day. Although it was Saturday, with the owner's deadline approaching, they'd probably been worked hard. And perhaps even understood there would be more work in the morning. One palomino mare lifted her head and cocked her ear, not as confident as the others that the ordeal was over for the time being. Rhue kept his eye on her as the others shifted to the far side of the corral.

Behind him the screen door swung wide and new boots struck the wooden porch, then dulled with the hard ground. Joey Clark's son stopped before he reached Rhue. If Rhue remembered right, the kid's name was Edward. It was too formal and not at all right for the hustler he looked, with his tight jeans and his T-shirt sleeve rolled over cigarettes to advertise the impunity of youth. He looked so young that the corral dust seemed to sit like powder on his five o'clock shadow. Hard to believe he was old enough to shave.

The boy tapped one boot sideways against the post. "D'you need a ride? I'm headed to town."

Town. It was like a mantra for these boys with its neon lights and parking lots squeezed so full of metal and hormones and hope that the energy shot out like headlights into the night. Rhue had been there. He had no desire ever to spend a Friday night on the town again. Even the memory of golden whiskey bleeding down his throat didn't tempt him.

"I could drop you somewhere," the boy repeated. He wasn't much more than a boy.

"I've got my truck." Rhue didn't mean it as brag. There was nothing in town for him anymore.

Edward Clark looked around and shrugged when he didn't see the truck, as if Rhue's version of things was unreliable under any circumstances. "Fine. See you."

When the kid didn't say tomorrow, Rhue wondered, was it disrespect or caution that kept him from that kind of promise?

The evening breeze carried the scent of the humans across the lane. When it reached the horses, one of them whinnied. Rhue hoped it was the palomino mare. Because he felt Edward's eyes on his back—suspicious, distrustful of an old man's reserve—he didn't move to the fence until the boy's truck rolled out to the state road. The horses waited too. Wild as they were, they were more polite than humans.

"Just you and me, babe," Rhue said to the mare as he squeezed between the rails.

Once he was in the corral, the fence at his back, the other horses pranced and prodded each other, showing off. Just beyond stroking distance, the mare darted away, enticing him to follow. He patted the few who let him, the older ones who connected him with carrots and apples, the ones who'd already accepted the bridle and their own talent to carry human weight. The new foals were too wild for that. They bucked and nipped each other's flanks. Where the fence widened, the gate stood open to the prairie. So, it was Saturday night. The ranch hands anticipated a late night and were letting the horses have their freedom too.

When Rhue walked past the oldest stallion, several of the

horses moved alongside him, but no longer within reach as if the open field granted them dispensation from protocol. The stallion stood motionless. Only the silk of his withers rippled in the dusk. Rhue imagined that the stallion had given orders. He'd forbidden the others to follow the human. Perhaps a Pied Piper fear, but the whites of the stallion's eyes shone wildly where he meant for them to stay clear. In transparent rebellion the palomino held herself apart, her breathing calm and measured.

"Come on then," Rhue answered and continued to pick his way through the tufted grass.

She sprinted past him then a furlong or two, spun around on a hillock of grass, and lifted her feet daintily, setting them down in the exact same spaces as if she were a new ballerina standing on tiptoes with excitement. When he realized he was holding his breath, he let it out in a long slow whistle. This was real. He could feel his own mood lift from the graveside fantasy of bottomless holes and ethereal mourners. The mare's nostrils blew warm air that misted in the cool evening. It floated back to him, a caress. Although she kept her distance, when she saw him struggle at the incline, she slowed.

Once he made the crest, she took off running into the wind. He wished he were astride her, the smooth sureness carrying him forth. It was an old ache, buried deep inside, recognized only in the instant when she'd whinnied. It had been a long time since he'd ridden. As his boots hit the hard shale of the rise, with the angle and the unforgiving ground, a sharp, piercing pain tweaked his hip joint. He stopped and let it run through him until it passed. Forty years ago he never would've noticed it.

Back then he'd been too busy. He'd ignored all the rules. With a rigor sprung from admiration, he'd volunteered to school the wild ones. It had made his reputation with the ranchers; an easy life for someone who had no schedule, no place he had to be, no one expecting him at home. Putting himself out for the horses had come naturally. The ranchers knew it, recognized that he had no hidden agenda, no other passions. Although their curiosity sometimes tied them up in knots over his refusal to answer questions beyond breeding and training, they didn't complain. And they paid him well for the answers he was willing to give.

The young cowboys, Edward Clark and the others—their legs practically growing longer as they strutted across the paddock—didn't understand either, but they were more aggressive and they wouldn't let it alone. They accused him of being sentimental, too patient with one horse, too tough on another. Rhue never bothered to explain. Each horse was different. Like women. Each horse yearned for its own space at the rail. Once he figured out what made a particular horse tick, he changed the routine to fit her desires. To him, it was common sense. And the horses eventually came around. He didn't have as much luck with women.

As he walked in the well of grass, the route to water worn by the herd, he remembered other evenings when he'd nestled into a mane and let hooves ring clear up to the sky, a prairie carillon of joy. Against the sinking sun the mare's silhouette held fast. She wasn't ready to give up the unknown night or the secrets that hovered at the far side of the meadow, the possibilities of surprise that existed nowhere else in the daily routine of horse and cowboy. Rhue laughed. Neither was he.

The pasture fell away, downhill for two or three hundred yards. A natural swale separated the bigger field from a second ridge that hugged the river. It was a lazy river, not wide enough or deep enough to make any kind of mark on the world, but steady enough to be noticed and named.

When he lost sight of the mare over the ridge, he panicked, moving faster. He didn't want it to be over. He called out to her, naming her as he spoke, "Delilah." He hoped she'd recognize her new name and wait. Just beyond the ridge he could hear stamping hooves and marveled that they'd reached the water without distraction. Horses had an uncanny sense of rightness in their movements. If the sky darkened or the wind brought a strange smell, they hesitated and evaluated each signal before moving on.

Humans, fools all, had no such warning system. They bounded ever onward toward an unarticulated goal or fantasized glory, dragging their silly paraphernalia with them, getting slower and slower until they died, surrounded by things that had no lasting value and by people they didn't love. That's why he'd never gone back east, to the slow, dull pain of living with neighbors who knew your past.

He liked to imagine Adriana throwing the things he'd left behind in the landfill, making a clean break. More likely— knowing her—she'd kept them as symbols of his betrayal. At the beginning in all that icy anger she might have hoped he'd return for his things so she could berate him for their paucity. Surely she would have worked hard with their son Ford to dispel any romantic hopes he might harbor of being restored to his father someday.

Although Ford was a man now, the name conjured the boy Rhue would have taken on his shoulders and wheeled about, not to show off, but to share the exhilaration of wide spaces and endless motion. He didn't know much about his son, hadn't asked out of fairness. He'd been the one to leave after all. But he would've liked a photograph, a small reminder of a reality that existed some distance from the very different life he'd made here. In the early years whenever he saw a child Ford's age, he would imagine how his son might have looked, a combination of her steadfastness and his yearning. It wasn't much of a legacy.

He tread carefully on the uneven ground. "Delilah," he let the words fly with the breeze. When more than one whinny floated back in reply, he grinned. They hadn't forgotten the human at their flank. Horses had a singular sense of cooperation in their separateness, something he'd always admired about them.

It had been a year, maybe more, since he'd walked this far. Arthritic joints and the odd collection of rodeo fractures discouraged hikes. The immediacy of Vince's death heightened his sense of aloneness. Although it bothered him that it bothered him—he hadn't gathered friends like trophies as other men did—it wasn't the physicality of being alone, but the sense that time had run out. He would be next, and who would bury him?

Behind the setting sun, the sky flamed with sulphuric borders of blue, a sure sign that a storm was on its way. He figured they had an hour or two before the rain hit. His bones confirmed it.

Mostly the wind blew from the west here, flowing down from the mountains and gathering speed to the Mississippi. Except for tornados and the pressurized summer storms, the weather was clear or clouds, nothing in between. Clouds meant stretches of drizzle for days. One time he'd ridden from Montana to Texas in steady rain, the horses' backs blackened with it, the mountains obscured in endless gray. Out here a man could get lost in the weather.

As he followed the palomino, his shirt stuck to the small of his back despite the rising breeze from the coming storm. When the mare caught his scent, she lifted her head. Already finished with her drink, she bobbed and tucked her head like a coquette with a new suitor. She knew he'd come for her.

"Hey," he said, patting his thigh with one hand to let her know he was real.

A few of the horses trotted out knee deep. After one lone filly neighed from the shoreline, a young stallion, barely that, came back for her. He nudged her along, first one flank and then the other until she melted into the herd, halfway across the stream. Stepping out of the water, Delilah nosed around the scrub that grew at the high-water mark.

"No use my telling you what a beauty you are," Rhue said out loud. "I won't be the first."

Although she'd been ridden before, you wouldn't know it from the way she hung back. He'd watched the boys train her. Too proud to go easily, she'd thrown a few cowboys before they realized she only wanted to be treated like the lady she was. If they showed her the halter, let her take her time, she didn't complain. But she withheld something. In the way she refused to come for sugar, and in the slight hesitation before she let herself follow their signals, he guessed she didn't really like these humans who'd forced her to bend. Some horses craved attention and others never came in out of the weather. He could spend a lifetime wondering why or he could accept the difference.

He kept up a stream of sweet talk as he sidled down the rock face, his boots turned into the hillside for purchase. "If I were younger, I'd take you south, babe, past Texas—now there's a flat, greedy country without class—to Mexico. River valleys that make you thirsty just thinking about them. You don't know peace 'til you've been there." With his eyes on the mare, he willed her to be patient, to let this work. He wasn't sure he'd ever wanted anything more.

Besides Marian, there'd been women he'd talked to this way, low and dreamy, afraid to frighten them with his calloused hands and his appetite for change. Tiny women with rosy nipples and soft flesh, women who didn't know what they wanted. And tanned women with leather vests straining at the buttons and muscular thighs made for love. Women whose memories of men colored them angry, but their bodies were still wanting and needy. Women he'd loved but never told them, and women whom no one could love for long.

A horse was different. Once a horse knew you and knew what kind of man you were, it either liked you or it didn't. They never forgot you. And once you'd seen a horse, you couldn't stop dreaming of her. That's the way it was for him with Delilah. Even though the ranch hands treated him respectfully to his face, they'd already given him up for dead. Too old to sit the wild ones, too worn out for anything useful, he was allowed to water sometimes. It was the natural order of things. Delilah, though, didn't know he was old. She only knew he was interested.

Close to the bottom, where the shale unraveled into loose gravel, his boot caught and he skidded, a foot or so, landing on his tailbone. "God damn it to hell," he muttered, angrier when she stiffened at the abrupt motion. Her nostrils flared. His hip felt out of whack. Something had wedged itself in his chest. Slowly in order not to spook her, he twisted his arm and leg on that side to loosen the tightness. Bit by bit, as he continued talking and righted himself, she relaxed. When he edged closer, she stood motionless, eyeing him, but checking the other horses as if preserving her choice.

On the far embankment the sun tanked behind the trees, streaking its last heat into the clearing in greedy golden fingers. With his handkerchief freed from his back pocket, Rhue wiped his hands where they'd picked up gravel slivers from the fall. All of a sudden he was uncomfortably hot.

"Are we friends yet?" he asked, but stood his ground. "You're right, you're too young for me, but . . ." How to tell her there was value in experience, in being old enough to discard the tricks and deceptions of youth. How to let her know that he wanted what she wanted, one last glorious flight across the plain before the storm sent them home.

"A hundred miles south of the border—if you and I were traveling together—there's a canyon nestled into the mountains that come from California. Narrow, until you're actually inside, then you see the spring. Must be fifty shades of green 'round that spring." The words were low and even. "And in the meadow there's more ponies than I've ridden in my life. I'll bet you've got family there."

He inched forward, sloughing his boots through the sand, close enough that he could see her eyelashes. An arm's length between them. In her mane white hairs twisted together with the toffee. Years ago they'd had white horses at the ranch. Perhaps he'd ridden her forbearers, though he could see nothing familiar in the way she held her head assessing this bold human.

"The water there," he continued, "is like mountain water, cool and clear. You wouldn't mind that, eh?"

With a single slow sweep, he raised his hand to waist height and held it out to her. To keep his voice low and steady, he had to regulate his breathing. His chest ached from the forced control. There was no outcropping or birch to lean against. Past Delilah, the other horses churned about in the stream. Some had returned to the shore where they milled in circles, growing anxious with the deepening dusk. These next few seconds were crucial. If she were bored, she'd step back, abandon him. If she leaned in to smell, he'd know she was serious too.

His extended hand grew heavier and heavier in the chilly air. On the far bank the leaves rustled. He closed his eyes and sent her brainwaves of desire.

Just there on his palm, he felt the air first. Not nuzzling exactly, but exploring, wondering. This was an introduction, a kiss on the cheek at meeting. It meant nothing, committed no one, but it offered something more. He imagined her neck stretched out to his fingers, the dark lines of sweat on her coat from her run here, the stiff ears pricked to catch any change, any danger. Even the idea of opening his eyes risked the most miniscule sound, a shift that might send her frothing into the river. The sound of air, steamy in the dry dusk, flowed in and about the two of them locked in concentration as fierce as any embrace.

His hand wavered where he held it open. When her lips bumped his palm, he steadied it quickly before she could flinch. Her warm breath poured into his hand, a gift, a bond.

"Delilah," he whispered, and she stepped forward.

Chapter Two

*F*ord figured his mother would go ballistic when she discovered he'd been through the boxes in the attic labeled, 'Rhue.' He hadn't told her the house had sold. It had been hard enough convincing her to move to the nursing home. Why had he never looked through the attic when he was younger? It wasn't as if she'd hidden the boxes. He remembered playing cowboys and Indians in the attic, the perfect mountain hideaway in the Long Island suburbs. He'd probably stood on those exact boxes while he shot savages through the attic window.

In one box under a stack of starched dress shirts and a barely touched Holy Bible, he'd found an album of photos. It was this box, opened and immediately shut, that he had saved on moving day, carried it out to his car, looking over his shoulder as if it were contraband, and taken it to his apartment. He'd promised himself he'd sort through it the first rainy Saturday, and it had been ten months before he had the courage to open it again.

The photos fascinated him. In most of them his mother, younger, radiant, held hands and laughed, very different from the serious, formal woman he knew. And his father—the first picture Ford had ever seen because his mother had been so careful—with piercing brown-black eyes, draped his arm confidently about the woman who looked only at him in spite of the friends who crowded around them.

There was one photo of his parents, barefoot, eyes closed, dancing on a patio, the lampposts in the corners with their faint glow like aging fireflies. He wondered who could have taken that picture, who would have been a close enough friend to have been present at so personal a moment. In another more formal photo his parents posed in front of a white house with green shutters. The man squinting into the sun looked like his father but with gray at his temples—perhaps his father's father.

While his mother had insisted his grandparents had known him as a toddler, Ford had only one vague memory of wide hands that pinned him in place so he couldn't reach his mother and a freshly painted porch that glistened in the bright sun. The smell of paint, Old Spice, and perspiration were all mixed up in the memory.

His mother thought it must have been the country club in Connecticut, a Sunday afternoon when the senior Hogans had insisted she bring Ford to celebrate his third birthday. She had hugged the old man for a long time; that Ford remembered because he'd never seen her hug a man. And when, at thirteen or fourteen, he described the memory for her, she excused herself and went to her bedroom. Even through the closed door, he heard her crying. It was the first time he'd realized that his actions affected her happiness, the first time he'd understood the weight of responsibility that arose from relationships.

It was odd that his mother had never thrown away the boxes. They'd never been opened either. From the packing tape seams, still in place and set in such confident right-angled lines, they announced to any onlooker that the contents were meant to stay inside. The things in the boxes couldn't have meant anything to his mother if she'd never opened them. He couldn't begin to guess the meaning of play programs and books with margin notations in handwriting he didn't recognize. And even if they once meant enough to his father to box them up, they'd been rendered meaningless if he'd never sent for them.

But the pictures shocked Ford. It was like looking at an old-fashioned version of himself, costumed for a time machine. Rhue wore a different suit in each picture; all the lapels broad and out of fashion. He had a beard in most of the photos. In all Ford's fabrications of a father, the images rising from his mother's bad-day rants, he'd never imagined a beard.

Here was a puzzle, starched shirts and striped ties with that beard. In rare weak moments his mother had criticized Rhue as selfish, immature, but never a daredevil. She'd never hinted at that grin from the photos that said, "I may live with a pregnant wife and work in an office like the rest of you, but I don't belong here."

His mother was seventy-nine now. A survivor of one heart attack and a minor stroke, she was too old to upset with questions about a man she'd never forgiven. For her, Rhue Hogan didn't exist. Ford, though, was glad he'd found the photographs. They were a link to an unknown past, though he was damned if he was going to let the grinning man get away with that easy likeability.

When the doorbell rang, he was slow to answer it, deep in thought about a bearded Rhue and what would make a man like that leave a pregnant wife.

"Hey. Anybody in there?" an unfamiliar female voice called through the apartment door.

Still thinking about his parents, he opened the door. Before he could see who it was, the strange woman was inside. In that split second he took in the ragged blue jeans, frayed cuffs overlapping painted toenails, the oversized velvet shirt with mother-of-pearl buttons, and the irreverent saffron beret. She belonged to a decade long past, one she hadn't been alive to experience, but she didn't look dangerous. She streamed past him and straight to the windows.

"Is there a fire?" he asked.

"A comedian, just what I need when I've locked myself out."

"You live here?"

"Sublet from Angela Tocchio."

He knew he hadn't seen her before, but that left nothing else to say. He had no idea which apartment belonged to Angela Tocchio. He and Angela had spoken twice on the elevator. About the Yankees. She was a rabid fan and he preferred the Tour de France. The new tenant didn't look like a baseball aficionado, though.

"You can't conjure a key to my apartment, can you?" she asked. Her smile broadened and she tilted her head as if she doubted he could do anything of the kind.

"Depends."

"Now there's an original line. Don't tell me women around

here fall for that." She dumped two overflowing bags of groceries on his sofa and twirled back toward him, where he was still holding the doorknob. The top of her head ended at his chin. Her eyes were green and hazel, quirky but surprisingly restful.

"Begging your pardon," he waved to get her attention after she slid around the sofa and back to the window like a chameleon to the sun. "But I don't guess people can tell you much."

She turned around, frowning. When she continued to look confused, he peered into the hallway to be sure there was nothing else to follow. Still not confident there wasn't a trick in all this, he didn't shut the door. She had her hands on her hips. He wanted to laugh at the mimicry in it, but she looked so serious.

"Depends on what?" she asked.

"Which apartment is yours? I have keys from several past tenants." He winked, "For cleaning ladies."

"I bet your mother thinks you're cute."

He tried to ignore her as he rummaged in a cigar box from the bookshelf. Even across the room he could smell lemon—soap maybe, not strong enough for perfume—and the singular bright odor of laundry hung in the sun to dry. While she cruised the room and examined everything, he lined up six keys on the coffee table, some rustier than others, each attached to a different key chain.

"There you have it, the sum total of my love life. Eighteen years' worth of attempts at understanding the other half."

"210?" she asked without turning from the bookcase where she held to her ear the conch shell he had just bought at the city market.

He bent to examine the keys and selected one, with a feather for a key chain.

Like a small child she put the shell back, nudged it into place, and patted it. At the silence she twirled to face him again and when she saw the key, she clapped her hands. "Was there someone in 210 before me you loved?"

"I wish you'd said it the other way around."

That time she laughed right out loud. He tossed her the key.

"I must live right," she said and disappeared through the open door before he could ask how long she'd be staying in 210.

When he left for work, the feather and key had been slipped under his door with a note on sky blue paper, "Just in case it happens again. Evie Newton."

After ten hours at the lab Ford locked up and started home. Late shift meant the sidewalks were less crowded, no families, only couples on their way to fancy dinners and some single worker bees like him, headed home. This late-night walk was one of his favorite things about the lab job. The city at night felt different, looked different. Fewer cars, no anxious businessmen glued to cell phones. On the side streets he could swing his briefcase with no danger of injuring anyone. Often he paused at the windows of stores he would never enter in a million years. Manikins in smart strapless gowns or bikinis. Arrays of silver watches and diamond rings for the kinds of brides who would call it off if the caterer they wanted weren't available. Sometimes it took him two hours to walk the twenty blocks, but the fantasy city that existed only at night entranced him. Daylight he saved for errands and exercise.

He stopped for sushi. Another good thing about the city; in any other town they would have closed hours earlier. While he ate, he read the paper. The news rarely surprised him anymore. The same old wars simply appeared at new latitudes. Photos of politicians and football players were interchangeable. In the book review section he found an article about a man who'd sailed around the world. Ford bent the newsprint margin to the edge of the table, tore it off, and stuck it in his wallet.

The ocean—its moods, its vastness, the shifting shallows, and the unexplored depths—had always fascinated him. It contrasted so sharply with his shoulder-to-shoulder days, the biting city wind with all its homeless flotsam. He carried with him the idea of the ocean, the enticing continuity of sea and sand like a lucky penny, a talisman of sorts. So far the idea had been enough.

Perhaps his father had gone to the ocean when he left the city forty years ago. To a tropical island. Somewhere starched shirts weren't necessary and beards fit in, Ford bet. The sudden urge to know surprised him; the curiosity in itself, another puzzle.

Although it might risk his mother's anger, he decided to ask her what she knew. He stayed up later than usual to examine the attic photos. He made a list of questions about particular people in them. Even the rooms in the background might hold clues to the mystery of his father. After midnight he shuffled them all into a manila envelope to take to the nursing home, but the links he envisioned—grandfather, uncles, cousins—were faceless ghosts that tread heavily in his dreams. When the knocking started, he was still asleep.

"Just leave it," he called to the door, squinting in the glare. Noon-ish, he saw from the radio. He'd forgotten the alarm, so unlike him. It would be tight trying to squeeze in a subway ride to see his mother before work.

"It won't keep," the visitor said.

In the fuzziness of not enough sleep, he recognized his new neighbor's voice. "Ms. Newton?" He fumbled to free himself from the covers. "Bear with me, I'm not awake."

"You sound awake."

In double time he shuffled to the bathroom. He wasn't going to greet his new neighbor in complete disarray. He brushed his teeth, registering the mint sting only as he rinsed. When he splashed water on his bristled face, his father stared back at him. At least a man who looked like the attic photo. It was hard to assimilate, this sudden intrusion of a man who ought to mean nothing to him but was so fundamental to his existence. Did his father have running water wherever it was he'd gone? At forty it shouldn't matter, but the curiosity surprised him when anger wouldn't have.

Outside the apartment someone was singing. A mournful kind of folk song. Not any someone, but Evie, a woman who laughed with him, instead of at him. God help him if she liked country music. But the possibility she was here because she was interested in him made him smile back at himself in the mirror.

When he slid the dead bolt free, she stopped singing mid-phrase.

"What do the comedian and the hall gypsy have in common?" he asked.

Smiling as if she'd expected that particular question, she thrust a bakery box into his hands. "You saved my life yesterday."

He took the box and fingered the string knot. "Will it bite?"

"You look like you don't eat much fruit."

"Ah, Florence Nightingale. Not a gypsy at all."

"I'm late. If there are any left tonight, I'll stop and try one."

Before he could think of a way to keep her talking, she was halfway down the hall, the elevator door open. On her head she wore a kerchief like a flower seller from the street. As she fled, the tip of the orange cloth bounced up and down with her hair.

At the nursing home the shift supervisor accosted Ford. "Your mother didn't sleep well."

"Wasn't the doctor going to check her medication?" he asked, on the defensive.

"He said to buzz him when you came."

Around the corner Ford bumped into the doctor, hunched over the water fountain. Once the older man straightened, he pulled the white coat and his clipboard to his chest like armor. He spoke in a mumble of four syllable words, his eyes darting everywhere but Ford's face.

"I can't do that medical jargon," Ford said, ashamed at the inability to hide his impatience with the man responsible for his mother's care, "Can you translate into plain English, please?"

"She's not responding to the treatment. But you knew that."

"Her kidneys again?"

"Very typical. She's retaining fluid, like she did last winter. But her heart's too weak. There's not much we can do except make her comfortable."

Ford wanted to ask how much time she had, but the doctor's awkwardness explained it all. No answer would solve the problem. Ford found her in the garden room, tucked into her wheelchair with several Crayola blankets—he swore they did that to fool the patients into thinking happy thoughts—and a single daisy in her lap.

"Mom?" When she didn't wake up, he stroked her sleeve and her eyelids fluttered open.

"Did you lose your job?" she whispered, the words an effort.

"Why would you think that, Mom? I work evening shift, remember?"

"You have dirt on your face."

"It's a beard."

Her lower lip drooped in surprise. He couldn't remember when he'd surprised her like that.

"Well, the beginning of a beard," he explained, dragging one of the heavy vinyl chairs closer to her wheelchair. "I found some old pictures of . . ." he hesitated. Dad sounded too intimate for someone he'd never met. ". . . of Rhue."

"Who?" she asked. It was Dr. Seuss laughable for as long as she'd carried the grudge.

"Rhue. My father, your husband." Blurted out like that, it sounded harsh but an odd urgency cramped his usual reticence. "You never told me why he left."

"He never said." This was the bitterness he'd seen in the stiff line of her jaw when, as a boy, he did something wrong or disappointed her.

"Mom, I'm forty. He's been gone longer than that. Can't you just give me the facts?"

"Whose facts? It won't make any difference."

"I'm asking, Mom. Please."

"What there is . . . it's all in the boxes," she managed after a bit. Working her jaw and her lips, she made the shapes of words but no sounds emerged. Like a blacksmith's bellow, when the air had worked itself through the system, she spoke again, raspier still. "He wasn't ever really here. Oh, we lived together for a year before the wedding and some time after that. He signed the marriage license, put up with the ceremony, but his spirit was . . . out there."

After she waved both arms in a wide circle, she erupted in sputters that turned into a cough. She huddled into herself. He patted her back.

"Out there?" he pressed. He saw the undefined horizon of the ocean, a line that intersected nothing.

In spite of her nap she was tiring. "I had a postcard once. From South Dakota, I think. Utah, maybe."

With one hand under the other elbow she reached up and pushed the hair off her forehead in a gesture so familiar Ford thought he might cry after all. Something about her frailness now after the years of fierce independence made her seem so vulnerable. He'd never thought of her that way.

A line of trees flanked the wall of windows and the afternoon sun blared between the branches. It made the room unbearably warm. She began again. "He called one time. Wanted to know what I'd named you."

"When was that?"

"The year you were born."

He didn't have the heart to make her look at the pictures.

When he arrived home from work, Evie was ensconced in his apartment. The living room smelled like a coffee shop. Several books, spines cracked, lay on the floor beside her; Lewis and Clark, displayed in her lap

"You left it unlocked," she said, her mug held aloft in invitation.

He put his briefcase in the corner. "I don't mean to be rude, but I can't drink coffee. It's hard enough for me to sleep."

"Guilty conscience keeps you up?"

"Kind of," he said as he retrieved a half-drunk water bottle from the fridge. "Is all this . . . ah . . . generosity because of the key?"

"Yesterday you looked like you'd just lost your twin brother to cancer," she said, but he wasn't sure he heard it correctly because he was so busy watching her lipstick leave its imprint on his favorite mug.

"My father," he said.

She sprung up and moved toward the door. "God, I didn't mean to pry. What a jerk. I'm really sorry. Why didn't you just tell me to go jump in a lake?"

He stifled a guffaw at the fierceness of her reaction. "Not cancer, just simple abandonment. No big deal. It was forty years ago, but I never knew for sure until yesterday."

She sat back down. "If he's the one who left, why are you feeling guilty?"

"Are you a shrink?"

"Sorry. Natural curiosity. I'm a voyeur. Can you tell?"

"Better than a gypsy, I guess."

For weeks they bumped into each other—in the elevator, on the front sidewalk, or at the corner convenience store—sometimes full of things to say and sometimes silent. He didn't mind the silence, but he would have liked to know if she did. He wondered about her age, where she went during the day, about the rings she wore in wild array but only on one hand, and about the easy friendships she struck up with the other tenants, people he'd passed on the stairs for years without knowing their names.

He didn't ask any of these questions. Mostly because she directed their conversations and he enjoyed the unpredictability. She was preoccupied though with an old boyfriend who wasn't giving up. Several nights she came in after Ford had been home from work for an hour or so. Through both closed doors and across the hall he could hear her arguing on the phone. The strain of restraint was clear even from that distance. The third time it happened he decided she might need someone to listen. Changing back into his jeans, he knocked and asked her if she wanted to watch a movie on late-night TV. She said no, but thanked him with a peck on his cheek. Her face had been blotchy and flushed. She'd been crying, he guessed.

He stayed up until three, writing and rewriting a funny note to distract her, which he ended up not giving her after he found out by accident from the landlord Maurice that she was only twenty-four. Sixteen years of striking out wasn't much to offer someone with that much of a future.

On the nights she wasn't upset by the boyfriend, they talked over beer or hot chocolate about everything except relationships. One evening, in the middle of a sentence, she fell asleep on his sofa. He covered her with a blanket and went to bed, only to find that he couldn't sleep. The ceiling, dancing with city lights, reminded him of his childhood bedroom—a connection he'd never made before. He lay awake admiring the man-made borealis.

Except that somewhere in that serene appreciation, an overwhelming sadness descended. The whirls and flashes reminded him of the Christmases and birthdays his mother had ignored in purposeful and furious counterpoint to any feeling she ought to overdo, to make up for his father's omissions. And for the first time he recognized how lonely it must have been for her. How easy it was to fill up a life without curing the loneliness.

When the nursing home doctor telephoned and asked for a face-to-face conference, Ford requested the day off.

His boss grimaced. "You're expendable, you know."

The day before the appointment the nurse called Ford's apartment again and woke him up. "Your mother's asking for you."

"Is she all right?"

"If she were my mother, I'd come right away."

After taping a note to his door for Evie, he spent the extra money for a taxi, then lost his temper with the driver who didn't appear to understand, "Hurry, please." As the cab parked at the main entrance to the nursing home, they were loading his mother's stretcher onto the ambulance. On the narrow bench beside her he rocked with the city traffic and held her hand, more fragile than he remembered from his visit four days earlier.

This is a moment that comes to everyone, he thought. This is life, the natural order of things. I ought to be more ready than the next guy, having done without one parent from the start.

In between deliberately indistinguishable assurances, he pattered on about nothing and tried to think what he ought to tell her if this were it. Although the oxygen mask hid her expression from him, he was sure she could hear him. She squeezed his hand. He was remembering a day she had taken him to the beach. He'd been five, maybe six, the salt spray in his eyes and the edgy feeling of pushing against the powerful waves to stay upright. She'd paced the beach, reminding him of the dangers in shrieks that were swallowed by the wind. When he'd finished and been dried off with a towel bigger than he was, she hadn't let go of his hand again. They'd only gone that once.

"Don't die," he repeated over the muffled traffic noise outside the ambulance, with the same ineffectiveness.

At the hospital they wouldn't let him stay with her until he filled out every last admission form. By the time they were reunited, he was hoarse from arguing. Tubes and machines surrounded her. The industrial wall clock's minute hand ratcheted around more than once. Without any attention to the hours and only a slight startling at the mechanical catch every sixty seconds, he watched her sleep as if it were necessary to memorize each minute detail for an exam of epic proportions.

At the end though, she was lucid. "I loved you more," she said, and he knew what she meant.

By the time Evie arrived, having tracked him down through Maurice and then the nursing home receptionist, he was asleep on the empty chair outside the room where his mother had been. He signed the last form and they walked the thirty blocks back to the apartment.

"Odds are they fired me at the lab today," he said.

"Funny, I was thinking about taking a trip, but I fall asleep driving when I'm by myself." She swung her arms so that their shoulders bumped in a gentle rhythm that matched his steps.

"Far from here?" He could hear the forlorn tone in his voice and looked beyond her so she wouldn't see it in his eyes.

"More like to somewhere."

The lab director let Ford go, with a leave of absence. "Family leave," Jonathan Grabeel snorted. "Thank the Democrats." He edged off the stool, abandoning the microscope. " Six weeks max. Give me two weeks' notice when you're back and we'll find a place for you." He was trying to smile, but it was not something he did often and it was an obvious struggle. "Depends on the grant funding, goes without saying."

"Of course," Ford agreed and cleaned out his locker, just in case.

On his way out Jonathan stopped him again. He simply planted himself in Ford's path as he reached for the door. "Sorry about that 'being expendable' comment last week. I was having a bad day."

The thunderstorm that had been threatening for hours let loose as they walked together to the elevator. The lights in the hallway flickered, but were restored before either could comment. Although an expression of sympathy from the man would have cemented the job's reservation, Ford did not expect one. Neither of them had shared their private lives—his mother's last illness was his first request for time off—and the painstakingly detailed lab work did not lend itself to casual conversation.

As the elevator doors slid shut, he heard the director over the whir of the cables, mumbling as if to himself. "Sorry about your mother too."

Jonathan's regret and Ford's own colored the afternoon and the bus ride back to the apartment. More than the heat that pressed in on all sides and the black clouds that shadowed him, Ford felt an opportunity had been lost. They were similar in temperament, each committed to the scientific method, each more interested in the lab than current events or office politics. Ford promised himself, when he returned, he would ask Jonathan to lunch.

He and Evie packed enough clothes for two weeks, figuring if they stayed longer, they'd find Laundromats when they ran out of clean things. For Evie, it was everything she owned: at least that's what she told him. She hadn't lived long enough to accumulate any significant amount. The recognition of that difference gave him second thoughts again. A bad experience might ruin her chances of ever finding the right guy. Here he was, a middle-aged research scientist, a creature of habit, dependent on books and solitary late night walks for adventure. What possible attraction could he be for her?

If pity motivated her, he needed to know now and end it before he made a fool of himself. But when she bought a huge flowered beach umbrella from the thrift store and a bungee cord to lash it to the car, talking her out of going became more improbable than their ending up together in the long run.

After several awkward sessions at the funeral home and the lawyer's office, where it was obvious they thought he'd lost it, he arranged for the burial of his mother's ashes in the Massachusetts coastal town where she'd been born. The discovery that he came from Puritan stock pleased him. To arrive in this country in the beginning when forests stretched to the mountains and there was no turning back, that would have been exciting. And it was reassuring to learn that pioneering was in his blood. Perhaps—the thought niggled in the back of his consciousness—that had been one of the attractions when his father had gone west.

His mother's ashes were transferred into an urn and he would deliver them himself. Dust unto dust. Evie had never been to New England.

"Did you pay your rent in advance?" she asked, her arms full of sleeping bag. Camping was a possibility.

He nodded as he shoved the folding chair from his bedroom into the back of the rented car. They had debated buy or rent—neither of them owned a vehicle—and had opted to stay flexible.

"Does Maurice have a key to your apartment in case there's a flood or something?" she asked.

He nodded again. Although Maurice had managed the building for a decade, Ford couldn't remember the specifics of any of their conversations, including the last one about the arrangements during his absence. Evie was already on a first-name basis with everyone.

"What about your plants?" she asked.

"They're not really mine. I inherited them from Caitlin."

"Caitlin?" She rolled her eyes, "Should I be jealous?"

"No. Two girlfriends ago."

"That's no reason to let them die from lack of attention. Maurice might water them."

"For a fee."

"I thought you said your mother left you some money."

"For the future, not to water plants."

"This is the future. You can't start a new life with murder on your conscience."

"Fine, I'll give them to Maurice."

"He'll love the thought, but he won't take them. He's more lazy than lonely."

"How do you know these things about people?"

Hooking a stray strand of black wavy hair under her beret, she smiled and kissed the knuckles on his hand where he held the door for her. "Everyone's lonely."

"Not me, not anymore."

Later, as he sat in the silent apartment on the radiator by the window that overlooked the street, waiting for her to return from saying good-bye to a sister he hadn't met, he knew he'd lied. When Evie was gone, he was miserable. The women he'd known trailed across his conscious mind, a parade of friends and lovers, probably more than he deserved for the distance he'd kept.

In high school he'd been shy, inept. Without initiating any conversations, but eager to learn their secrets, he'd watched girls at every opportunity, speechless when they wanted to borrow his homework or to be his lab partner.

In college, once he discovered that women could be enticed with deep issues and political fervor, he tried on philosophies and girlfriends like hats in a department store. The variety and breadth of this experience had exhausted him. One girl, after accusing him of never feeling true love, tried to light a fire in his library carrel. The struggle to stop her terrified him. To witness the power of love gone bad, to know that, despite his best efforts to remain unattached, someone had been driven to that level of despair over him, made him wary of any entanglements. He saw for the first time the wisdom of his mother's detachment. He swore off women.

Evie, though, had a matter-of-factness about her that was not threatening in the least. There was no desperation. She demonstrated no unpredictable swings from high to low. After the old boyfriend finally gave up, and even during that struggle, she'd maintained a calm acceptance of the rightness of her decision. Ford had heard her tell the man if he didn't wake up singing, this wasn't the right time and she wasn't the right person.

In the days following his mother's death, Ford thought about what Evie had said. Here was his chance at a new life. His mother's claim on his attention had ended. The anger she'd imposed on their life for forty years drained away. Immense relief flooded through him. If he met his father now, by chance or by design, at least there would be no guilty conscience, no anxiety over displaced loyalty to his mother.

And if he never met his father, he hadn't lost anything because he'd never had anything. His mother had given him that.

Chapter Three

When Rhue woke up, he was in a hospital room. A slender dark-skinned man in a white lab coat, clean-shaven, with gold spectacles like a professor, stood at the foot of his bed. Someone coughed next to him. A double, so it couldn't be ICU or the penitentiary. He tried to move his legs but they were pinned under the taut cold sheet. His head was propped at a slight angle and tubes ran from his chest and arm to machines between the two beds.

"What happened?" he asked. The words tripped over themselves and made an irritating echo above the air-conditioner revved into high gear. The Indian-looking man, intent on his clipboard, ignored him.

Rhue coughed on purpose. "What happened?" he tried again, pushing the sounds past his vocal cords with an effort that sent sharp spurts of pain along his ribs. He coughed for real.

"We're not sure." The East Asian accent was discernible. "You fell. Maybe a stroke or a small heart attack. Not unexpected for someone in your condition."

"What does that mean?"

"It means you're too old to be riding wild horses."

Rhue didn't remember riding the mare, but he hesitated to admit it. Memory loss might be something that would keep him here longer.

"What day is it?"

"Thursday, the 4th. Why? Have a pressing engagement?" The doctor laughed. When Rhue didn't laugh back, the doctor tweaked his tie, looked at his shoes, and then wrote rapidly on the papers stuck in the clipboard.

Three days lost, Rhue didn't think it was funny. "When can I leave?"

"We're not holding you."

Gripping the bed rails, he tried to sit up.

"But," the foreign doctor put a firm hand on Rhue's shoulder, pinning him to the pillow, "we can't tell you anything definite until the results come back." He shook his head in discouragement. "You're almost eighty. Even if it's just a broken bone, it means rehab and follow-ups." The words, as clipped and precise as a glockenspiel, were discordant high notes in the darkened room. "The tests won't be completed for another day or so."

When the patient in the next bed shifted and began a rough snoring, Rhue wondered if the man had been awake listening to it all, or if he were a coma patient, locked in a nowhere land. Rhue imagined a long hallway of rooms with bodies, motionless and barely breathing, lying in shallow hospital beds like corpses in a cemetery. With trembling hands he fumbled with the sheets to loosen his legs.

He sat up. It took less effort than he'd expected, considering all the equipment. His head felt so light that he had to put one hand on the bedrail and grip it to keep himself connected. With the other he touched the throbbing place on his jaw. In several places the skin on his face was tender. Somehow he must have scratched himself. His legs, numb and invisible under the pale green coverlet, remained dead weights. When he looked up at the doctor, he saw that the man was watching him as if he'd never seen such an intriguing specimen.

"What's the matter with my legs?"

"Nothing with the right one except bruises. On the left, one fracture, near as we can tell, close to your ankle. We've casted it, but it may need to be reset."

"If I don't wait, if I go now, what's the risk?"

"Ah, if I knew that, I'd be a fortune-teller, not a doctor."

After the cryptic little doctor left, three male nurses bustled in. The oversized one supervised the other two. They twisted Rhue from one side to the other, cast and all, and sponged his entire body with soapy water, then clean. They didn't speak to him except to explain each step. He didn't talk at all. The outrage of having someone do what he had been doing for himself for years hung heavier than the solid white plaster that clung to his left leg below the knee.

When they were done, they whisked him into a wheelchair,

flicked down the cream hallways to the elevator, and swished into a spacious white room. It was empty except for a metal tunnel centered over a low-slung conveyor belt. Stretching him out on his back on the stainless steel tray, they straightened his hospital gown and disappeared, this time without explanation, but with orders to stay perfectly still. To a droning hum, the tray inched him through the tunnel. If he'd asked, he supposed they would have told him what they were doing, but he was more worried about his inability to remember mounting the mare.

Thirty minutes later, back in his room they tucked him, clean and exhausted, into the narrow bed again. A young girl in a nurse's uniform spoon-fed him applesauce and lukewarm chili from a plastic tray. Once he finished eating, she excused herself to put the tray in the hall. He closed his eyes, still trying to remember Delilah and the wind by the river. Dozing, he lost track of time and place.

He traveled again, the long dry highway from Adriana and New York City to the Rockies. He'd been eager to distance himself from his own sense of failure. For the first thousand miles, the urge to disappear was so strong he'd been unable to eat or sleep. Her voice spoke from the crowds so often he had a crick in his neck from turning in surprise. The cities he'd traveled through had been glistening and glittery, mad with colors and people, whirls of activity. He'd fled, farther and farther west, looking for a place with a single color and no voices.

Trapped in the neatly bound hospital sheets, he dreamed of canyons roiling with wild ponies like the Canadian coast, where the tide turned in front of your eyes, churning the water into salt and spray. And he rode the train again across new countryside, forests as green as the underside of moss, the soil black with fertility and age like coal. The sky had been pale blue, frosted with stratus clouds so close to the edge of the atmosphere that they tempted you to reach up and push them over the edge, to clean house. And each farmhouse and ranch—expectant, windows lit, flags raised—stretched out across the country like parade watchers, cheering him onward to whatever was waiting for him, whatever it was that had made him leave everything he knew for nothing he could name, for the unknown, for the vacancy of open land and no neighbors.

He hadn't understood why the urge to escape had been so overwhelming. He'd been afraid to think about it.

Although he knew he'd dreamt, he had no recollection of it when he woke. As soon as he opened his eyes, the young nurse spoke as if on cue from the metal stool by his bedside.

"Next of kin?" she asked, her own eyes focused on her lap and the paperwork there.

"Doc didn't say I was dying."

"It's a routine question. Don't you want us to call someone?"

"I'm not going to be here long enough for cards and flowers."

She sucked at her pen like a lollipop. He watched her, sideways from the pillow where she'd cranked him down to sleeping position without asking. Her skin glowed pink at her cheekbones and paled at her forehead and jaw. The veins there pulsed steadily, thin traces of indigo visible through the smoothness. Without the dark eyeliner, he would have guessed she wasn't old enough to be away from her mother. He almost expected her to say, *Golly, Mr. Hogan, it's not that bad.*

"Don't you have a wife or a girlfriend?" she asked.

"Nope. Do you?"

"Oh, Mr. Hogan. You're being silly."

"I'm bored. I need to get out of here."

"You just went through a traumatic experience. You're supposed to rest."

He looked at her ponytail, with the pink ribbon that matched her sweater. He'd never been that young. "Are you even old enough to be a nurse?"

She giggled.

After she left, he limped across the room. The cast was awkward, but that had been anticipated by the doctor. Crutches stood guard in their pristine cardboard sleeve in the corner. In the narrow metallic closet, his blue jeans and his shirt hung stiffly as if they had suffered the same failure he had. When he put them on, they smelled of the open prairie and Delilah. Small tears like knife slices had appeared on one elbow and a button was missing. Buckling his belt, he caught a glimpse of himself in the mirror. Gaunt to the point of emaciation. Except for the hospital dinner—if you could call it that—he couldn't remember the last time he'd eaten either. No point really in trying to remember the three days he'd lost.

When he raked his fingers through the white hair, he could feel the plates in his skull. It was possible that the reverse of birth was happening without his knowing, that in the process of aging, the plates shrunk like everything else and your brain was exposed to injury again. It was a new thought in a chain of uncharacteristic thoughts, more introspective since Vince's burial, and all unsettling. There was that same sense of time passing too quickly.

The locker held no hat. He must have lost it on the ride.

In the hallway the solid stump on the bottom of the cast made a hollow pounding sound on the linoleum like a hammer on a neighbor's roof. The elevator, the woosh of the prairie breeze before the storm. Before the door shut, he looked back to see if they were following him, but the hall was deserted.

At the apartment he paid the taxi with money he found on his dresser. The steps from the street to the two rooms he rented behind the Laundromat had been easier to negotiate with the cast than he'd expected. To save Rhue the trouble, the driver had followed him in for the money. With the door closed and the whirring of the taxi's wheels against the wet pavement fading, he looked around the room where he'd spent the last ten years. Newspapers were strewn on the tables. Pots of caked dirt with brown stalks poked into the dry air, paper coffee cups littered the counter: all set down with the abandon of a chess game gone hopeless. It was not unlike places he'd lived in New Mexico and South Dakota. Except that he'd had better views.

Limping to the bedroom, he lowered himself to sit on the bed. Off balance, his toes scraped the closet door. When it swung open, dirty laundry and muddy boots littered the floor. The twang jolted all the way up to his hip.

"Damnation." He scrounged under the bed for the phone book. A vague recollection came back to him of kicking it there after that last conversation with the ranch owner. Supercilious and curt, the absentee owner had meant more than he said. Rhue bristled all over again at the insult.

On hold with the train station attendant while he checked the schedule, Rhue rummaged through the pile of mail on his bedside table. Without opening it he chucked most of it into the trash. His leg was throbbing. Once he had the information he wanted about the train, he hobbled to the bathroom and took four aspirin without water.

Three large trash bags later the room looked close to its pre-occupancy state. His duffle lay by the door. Taking the last beer from the refrigerator back to the bedroom, he lay down on the bare mattress, swung his bum leg up, and fell asleep.

After he signed in at the nursing home front desk the next morning, he limped along to Marian's room, the crutches safely tucked behind the receptionist's door. Someone had braided Marian's hair the way she liked it, loose twists in a long single strand down her back. He took her hands and waited for her eyes to focus.

"I'm going away. May not be back for a while. You'll have to keep everyone straight on this end."

She didn't smile or speak. He locked eyes and waited.

"Vince won't be by. He's already gone." No point in distinguishing between the two kinds of departures.

Twisting her fingers loose, she rocked in the wheelchair to the familiar hum, but stopped abruptly when he stood.

"Remember the palomino I told you about?" His voice was almost a whisper.

She sat motionless. The hub-bub of nurses and call buttons and elevator doors filled in the silence around them.

"Her name's Delilah."

Marian tilted her head as if she didn't believe him, but he'd seen that expression before when the staff tried to get her to eat or when Vince had started one of his stories, an old signal that she brooked no nonsense.

"I think you rode her once. Or her mother. Sixteen hands high, a slight hesitation in the right foreleg, maybe a snake bite. I'm not sure why I'm telling you this." He half expected her to start in with her own recollection of the mare.

A nurse passed in the hallway, with a long stare at the two of them as if she suspected he was getting ready to feed Marian pills to end it all. He stepped back, but kept his eyes on his friend.

"Anyway, she's out there. Didn't take much to me, but you, you could make it right with her." When Marian didn't acknowledge him, even with a hum, he turned away. "She's all yours. I have to go."

It was the best he could do. Vince would've made her laugh. But he already knew he was not great at good-byes.

At the bank in town the teller smiled. Her teeth were perfect.

"Good morning," her Texas drawl was a surprise here in the Montana hills. Flouncing her blonde hair off her shoulders, she waited for him to direct her.

He thrust the bank statement across the counter. With glossy pink nails she smoothed the crumpled page, examined the numbers there as if assessing him for marriage. When she looked up, her face was blank except for the tight smile that anticipated trouble.

"Is there a problem, sir?" she asked. Conscientiousness oozed from every Mary Kay pore.

"I want to close the account."

The woman looked over her shoulder. Licking her lips, she wiped the corners in a practiced pinch of those ringless pink-tipped fingers. "Are you dissatisfied with the way we've handled your account?"

The words were audible only to him as if the innuendo alone would collapse the bank around them, instantly and completely, rubble from the community tower that they'd been for their chartered one hundred years.

"Moving, that's all."

The smile reappeared in all its brilliance. A tiny silver glint far back in her mouth and he understood in that single glimpse that she loved sweets, kept the job for the dental insurance, and lived alone.

"Which bank shall I make the counter check out to?"

"Cash'll be fine."

She gulped, but somehow the smile remained intact. He could see the question—cash, why cash?—slide from her brain to her lips, but she didn't speak. A result of bank training, he guessed, and not her nature.

The duffle strap fit snugly into the ridge on his shoulder. Without the cumbersome crutches he could manage to stay upright if he leaned away from the bad leg and forced himself not to hurry. Walking past the dusty storefronts, he recalled aimless Saturdays here and endless late nights coming home from Tiara's Titty Palace on Roosevelt Street. Although the sidewalk was uneven, he knew the places to watch. Montana had been a fine place to live, though he'd liked Utah best. Fewer people, no people with questions.

He had propped the crutches at the drugstore's back door on the off chance that someone there might rescue them and send them back to the hospital. He didn't want the doctor to think he was ungrateful. At the train station he debated whether to pay the two dollars for a luggage check. Where the cast chafed, a blister was beginning and the train wasn't due until five: a long day for dragging around that extra weight in addition to the cast. Wrapped in a T-shirt, the money was buried at the bottom of the duffle except for a fistful of hundreds, which he'd put in a plastic bag and had slid inside the cast. Unwilling to risk the curiosity of the attendant, he hooked the duffle strap to his good ankle and shoved the bag under the bench.

With an old ten gallon from his closet tilted over his eyes, he dozed on the bench, half in and half out of sleep. He might have been able to maneuver the truck out to the ranch for one last conversation with Delilah, but so close to the weekend the owner was more likely to be there. No point in another argument when Rhue was leaving town anyway.

In his waking dreams Delilah held steady. She let him lift himself to her back and took him streaming across the prairie night, racing against the fading sun, not willing to yield to a strange voice. He forced himself to envision the rest. The image of himself aloft the palomino filled his mind and he slowed his breathing to keep the picture strong. By now the young stallion would have chosen. The shy chestnut mare, perhaps impregnated with his foal already, would stay close, her pace matched to his, following the grassy steppe to the river a half beat behind him. And from the ridge he and Delilah would watch them and remember their own courting days.

"Rhue?" A gravelly voice interrupted the dreams.

When he jerked upright, the cast crashed to the floor. He cut off the cry of pain and ground his molars to catch himself. His good leg, caught in the strap, wouldn't straighten.

Tiara put out a hand tentatively to help. "Rhue, honey, you're a mess."

"Thanks."

"Did your landlord throw you out?" She bent closer and pulled the strap free.

Her perfume, too strong for daylight, filled his lungs. Blinking in the noonday glare, he stifled a sneeze.

Her hand rested on his arm. "Do you need a place to stay?" And when he hesitated, she added, "Temporary, of course."

"I'm leaving on the train."

"You always said they were going to bury you here by the Tetons." She pouted as if that were her first choice for the day's activities.

Yet he wondered how she'd known he'd intended a one-way trip. When he didn't answer her, she sat down next to him and pointed to the cast.

"How d'you do that?"

He smiled.

"Riding one of those damn horses, I bet. You got no sense, Rhue Hogan. How old are you anyway? Too old for horses. Too old for moving on." She put her lips next to his ear. Soft, moist, he felt them brush his skin.

If she'd forgotten the last time they'd made love, he hadn't. Getting old, what a grand deception life was. Experience counts, they tell you all your life. So you gather it all in, a thousand experiences, building and building, stronger and smarter. Each event, each relationship makes you a better worker, a better friend, a better lover. But without the power of youth, experience counted for nothing. He could ride the palomino only in his dreams.

"Where you headed?"

He shrugged. Even before she'd asked, he hadn't been sure. The ticket said New York, but the train stopped a dozen places. He could get off wherever he wanted. He flashed the ticket at her and lay back down.

"What do you want to go back there for?"

He must have talked in his sleep. There was no memory of telling her about his wife—ex-wife—and his son. No reason to. His life back East was ancient history. When he still didn't speak, she grew impatient, flicking the cigarette ash in a careless arc and tapping her high heel shoe on the torn linoleum.

"It was pure coincidence I saw you through the window. You might'a got away without anybody to see you off." Her head circled around, an offhand effort to see if anyone had seen her talking to an old man on a train bench. "Well, that's it, I guess. If you're really going?"

He flashed her a wider smile. "Listen," he handed her the keys to his truck, "use the truck. The battery may need replacing, but it'll run for a long while yet."

"But, Rhue, honey, you can't be serious about not coming back?"

He thought she might cry then. She took a handkerchief from her purse but patted her nose and eyes instead. Replacing the handkerchief with a makeup mirror, she flicked blush on both cheeks with a tiny pink brush no bigger than her thumb. After applying fresh lipstick, she knelt down level with his face.

"I'll take good care of that old truck for you. You hurry back now."

He closed his eyes as if he were falling back asleep. When he heard the muffled sound of her heels on the sidewalk through the thick, netted station glass, he lifted the hat and checked his watch. One thirty-two, three more hours. He should take a walk, find some lunch, but the idea of going back down that sidewalk felt wrong to him. He'd already left this place.

Traveling east with the sunset behind him was comforting. The train's rocking motion put him to sleep again. When he awakened, he was ravenous, the hole in his stomach like a groundhog burrow, sudden and bottomless. He felt weak and dizzy. In the dining car a black-frocked waiter set a place for him with fresh linen. It wasn't a habit he was used to.

"Bourbon and water," he ordered.

"A double?"

"No, thanks." If he looked like he felt, no wonder the man thought he needed it. Outside the window the plains passed in the moonlight. Washed clean, the cool albino light made a widening beam on the open spaces like a fog light, illuminating bits and pieces of random civilization: barns and railroad crossing barriers and trestles over unseen rivers. As the soundless landscape fell away from the steady churning train, he turned melancholy. Without birdsong or radio or conversation the land could have been painted on the glass. It made Montana seem farther away still, and New York a total fantasy. Maybe Marian had the right idea, fade out before disappointment outweighed the rest.

When the steak came, he ate without pause. Beef juice leaked out in wide puddles and ran into his potatoes. He soaked the rest with his roll. The salt barely stung his lips where his perpetual sunburn was almost gone from being inside for days running. Like the mountains, it was part of the life he'd left. Still hungry, he ordered dessert, something he rarely did, something associated with the civilized life he'd rejected when he'd left the city.

For once in his life he left a large tip. The fellow hadn't bothered him with a lot of questions and he appreciated that. The time in the hospital might have weaned him from sun and wind, but he missed the constant motion of the horses. Because the train compartment was empty, perversely he wished for company. Someone quiet like Vince, who could tell a story with enough pauses to let you exercise your imagination.

In the blackness beyond the train, hulks of manmade buildings streamed by in between fencerows of spindly trees that looked like they'd been deprived of water and sun at the crucial moment. The farther east the train went the longer the stretches of buildings became.

At the Chicago stop he had an hour. To exercise his good leg, he walked the platform and read the newspaper headlines. He didn't stray far from the window through which he could see his duffle on the luggage shelf. A wagon vendor sold him orange juice in a tiny plastic bottle. Three swallows and it was gone. At the ranch they served pitchers of juice for breakfast and sausage links or slabs of bacon piled on platters, which the ranch hands passed in a rush. They'd all be snoring now, the single-width metal frame cots scattered every which way to catch what little breeze they could from the open windows.

Between two stretches of humming train cars, Rhue sat on a metal bench decorated with a rainbow of four-letter words and wondered what Vince was doing. If there were a heaven where life was the way you wanted it to be, would he choose horses again and open air? Where would Adriana and Ford fit in?

Unwrapping two ham biscuits from his backpack—rescued from the bottom shelf of his refrigerator—he ate them both, desperate suddenly for the salt. The hospital's list of restrictions, he recalled fleetingly with a glint of satisfaction, included pork. Inside the cast his leg felt feverish. Sweat dripped down, clinging to the plastic moneybag. Perspiration pooled there until it leaked past and down his ankle. The sock, rolled down to cover his toes, grew soggier and soggier until he couldn't stand it. He ripped it off. But when he stood to toss it in the trash container, he realized at the last second he might need it. It might be cooler in New York.

The Chicago station was buried underground. Like ants, red-capped luggage handlers and locals and tourists with too many suitcases scurried up and down the metal stairs. The whir was constant. After the warning whistle blew and he found his compartment again, he spread the wet sock on the radiator vent under the window. The combination of dinner, heavy and rich, and the salty ham biscuits sat on his stomach. Leaving Montana didn't seem like such a good idea anymore.

Chicago was a town he'd been through but never stayed in long enough to get to know. A long while back Tiara had hired a girl from there, with smooth smoky skin, her mood secretive and sensual. Without success he tried to think of her name, but even that remained suggestive, but indistinct. In the New York he remembered there wouldn't be any mysterious Chicago girls. Women in New York didn't like uncertainty. They wanted what they wanted. And they were singular in their purpose, inflexible and uncompromising.

A madam like Tiara would never make it in New York or Chicago, in any big city. Her heart was too soft, no matter how tough she tried to act. Holding his hand against the window, he tried to recover the sensation of making love to a stranger, the total freedom to be whoever you wanted for that particular moment without baggage or history. It crossed his mind that he might have a fever.

Once they left Illinois the train rattled through wheat fields interspersed with the backs of warehouses and short glimpses across gray water. Flotsam crowded the shore as if it would be glad to escape as well. There were more businessmen. They bellowed on cell phones and spread their computers on the empty seats. While they snored with the same intensity, Rhue borrowed one of their discarded newspapers and read the articles that went with the headlines. Nothing had changed in two days.

His leg itched maddeningly exactly where he couldn't reach it. Opposite his seat an overweight mother and her two pudgy children had squandered their money on junk food from the snack cart. Litter surrounded them like confetti. After they'd eaten everything, the boys proceeded to climb and tumble, bouncing from seat to seat in some kind of game only logical to children. Asleep finally in the empty seat between Rhue and the window, the younger child's sticky hand fell on Rhue's knee. The stubby fingers were pink and blue from the candy.

Rhue watched the boy's face as he slept. He'd never been this close to a child. Ford must have slept like this once, absent and yet overwhelmingly present in the intense quiet. Delicate veins decorated the child's eyelids. They flickered as if the images in his brain were too close or too graphic. Where his lips parted, sugary sighs wisped across Rhue's arms. Too short for the seats, the boy's legs dangled. His sneakers were smaller than Rhue's hands and swung with the train's motion.

As the child fell deeper into sleep, his head drooped sideways. Like a choreographed dancer in slow motion he drew his legs up and underneath himself, leaning and stretching until his head was in Rhue's lap. Rhue did not want to be rude. Although he cleared his throat, the mother was oblivious, entranced by a paperback book with a dripping dagger on the cover.

Because he was convinced waking the child would renew the earlier antics, he didn't dare move. The mother, though, had no such compunction. With loud rustles she gathered her handbag, scooped up a handful of trash from the floor, ordered the older son to stay put, and streamed off without looking back.

The weight of the little head on Rhue's legs hardly made an impression. Blinking in the weak compartment lighting, he stared across at the brother to be sure he had not imagined them both. It was amazing that a being that loud and energetic one minute could fall into repose so complete the next. Was the boy dreaming? Surely small children, retreating from a world where everything was bigger than they were, must dream. After he left New York, he'd never put much stock in dreaming. If you lived your life as you wanted, you had no need of dreams. A child, though, had no such power over the world. Only in his dreams could he run faster than his big brother, leave his bed unmade, and eat candy for breakfast.

The longer the mother was away, the more Rhue felt the importance of keeping the child asleep. Rhue had seen little children cling to their mothers. If the boy awoke while she was gone, he might panic. Without any firsthand experience Rhue had no idea what to do if that happened. The brother didn't look as if he would even notice. Moaning lightly—a monster in his dream?—the little boy curled up and burrowed into Rhue's lap.

"Did your mother say when she'd be back?" Rhue finally asked the older boy in as quiet a tone as he could manage and still make himself heard over the train clatter.

"Unh-unh." Shaking his head, the boy didn't look up from his comic book.

"Do you know where she went?"

"Unh-unh." Another anonymous shake of his head.

But for the sleeping child, Rhue would have taken the brother by the ears and lifted him off the seat to force a real answer. Instead his words whistled out in succession like darts. "Where did she go?"

When the older boy gave him a head-on stare the way a policeman asks for your registration and license with total assurance you'll obey without debate, Rhue gave up. To the timpani of metal wheels on iron rails, he considered the situation. Understanding the mother's need for relief and at the same time aghast at her willingness to trust a stranger with her children, he saw for the first time the enormity of what he'd forced on Adriana. While she had seemed to embrace it enthusiastically, maybe he had misread that too, and it had been a burden for her. His choice had narrowed hers.

The fact that he had never asked her what she wanted struck him as enormously selfish. He flushed, though there was no one there to see. She would be exactly correct to refuse to see him. Even if she'd been a better parent than he would have been, the fact that he hadn't even tried to understand what parenthood meant cut away at the sense of competence he'd built with the horses. Tiara had done more for her girls than he had ever done for anyone.

As the train pulled into the station, he stood, eager to escape, and carefully moved the boy's head to the cushion. At the last whining catch of wheel against brake, he bent down and whispered. "Your mother will be back in a minute. Your brother's right here." And he touched the older boy's shoulder. "You're in charge until your mother returns. Don't leave him."

Astride his duffle on the Buffalo platform, all his weight on the one boot, Rhue watched other travelers being greeted. They'd analyze each passerby with intense squints. When they realized the stranger was a true stranger, they'd shift their eyes up or beyond, turn their shoulders in rejection, not willing to acknowledge their desire, their need to connect. The chill of their separateness mingled with the stale smells of trash and engines and disappointment. Peering over shoulders and staring at overhead signs, the ticket holders dissipated in a long, slow drain until there were only two or three family groups left. They jostled each other, so glad to be reunited they weren't thinking of the next step, but reveling only in the touch and sight of their reclaimed kin.

When the last clump drifted off, Rhue stood alone on the empty concrete. The train steamed next to him, but he had half a mind to let it go on without him. The air smelled of burned grease and caked-on grit, so unlike Montana. He doubted he could get to a place here where the air would be only air and not a conglomeration of everything within twenty feet.

With his eyes closed he imagined himself back in such a place. He recalled the deep burnished thickness of the palomino's coat against the melting sun. She'd be tamed by the time he returned, if he returned. And if he found another wild one and rode her, there would be no one left to share it with. Then again, he didn't know anyone in Buffalo either.

The decision was suddenly easy. If he were abandoning Delilah and the plains he loved, he ought not to wander. He'd come for a reason. Even with second thoughts, the trip answered a void in his life created by Vince's death. Lugging the duffle back up the narrow metal steps, he was careful to find a different car in case the family was traveling east. He knew he wasn't reliable even if they didn't.

The truth was, and he could admit it now despite the sweaty grin of the older boy, he'd intended all along to find his son. The foreign doctor with his lyrical voice hadn't been too wrong. A stroke, lost memory, Rhue was old whether he liked it or not. There were things he would never see or do. And very little time to do what he had to.

As the train traveled eastward, it grew still more crowded. Across from him in the new car, two nuns sat side by side, their eyes bland and forgiving, their clasped hands frozen on their laps. He concentrated on the window, unsure what they were asking him with their silence and their assuredness. A thin woman in a raincoat that covered all but the tips of her fingers eyed the empty seat next to his. With the cast and all, he supposed he looked fairly safe. After much crunching and crackling of her shopping bag and several meaningful sighs, the thin woman managed to squeeze the bag under the seat. When she finally sat down, she tucked each side of her dress under her legs; he assumed in an effort not to infringe on his space. She ignored the crown of perspiration on her forehead, though it made him warm just to see it and he almost offered her his handkerchief. A worn cloth bag with a metal clasp stayed on her lap.

"Headed home?" she asked him after the ticket collector had passed. Finally she patted her face with a tissue drawn from the portmanteau.

"No, ma'am."

"Funeral?"

"No, ma'am."

"Job interview?" The skepticism in her voice increased with each question.

"No, ma'am," but he decided the remaining choices were too many and too absurd to perpetuate the conversation. "I'm looking for someone."

The plain woman clutched the tapestry bag on her lap tighter and leaned across it to speak. Her smile revealed crooked teeth. "Don't tell me you're a detective? I swear—well, I don't swear really, that's just an expression—I meet the most interesting people on trains. I'll bet it's a long lost heir. Millions of dollars waiting to free him from drudgery. Is that it? Or maybe a twin separated at birth? I think detecting is the most fascinating thing in the world."

"Nothing like that, ma'am. Just a relative."

"How long since you've seen him? Or her." She tucked a large white cloth, also drawn from the portmanteau, into the collar of her navy-blue dress. She was close enough for Rhue to see the pills of fabric where her sleeve had rubbed against the front of the cheap material. There was a neat but obvious mend where a buttonhole had unraveled.

Without waiting for an answer, she freed a glass jar from the bag and continued. "Care for some homemade watermelon pickle? It travels so well."

He couldn't imagine. Did she mean the jar? "No, thank you. I've eaten." The image of the two boys stuffing popcorn and gumdrops in their mouths while they hung upside down from the luggage racks returned. He stood up and pretended to stretch. The muscles in his good leg screamed from overexertion.

"How far have you come?" she asked, popping a second dripping pickle in her mouth. Her other hand, pinkie extended, held the cloth under her chin to prevent staining her dress, which in his opinion wasn't worth saving. Without waiting for an answer, she proceeded to tell him where she'd been and why.

The nuns were asleep; those vigilant eyes at rest. After a time, when he remained unresponsive, the solitary woman returned to her pickles. He felt a twinge of guilt. She was probably lonely.

He didn't know which was worse: gooey children or garrulous women. Marian would never impose herself on someone else's solitude. On cattle drives they'd ridden often eight, nine days without a single word, in charge of two hundred head. She'd been so independent and capable that he'd forgotten she was a woman. Forgotten until they returned to town and Tiara spun her web. Marian refused to countenance the easy slide into amorality that drew him to town after weeks on the open range.

"You must know what she has to do to get them to stay?" Marian argued. "She holds their money, pretending to be a friend, abusing their trust."

"Tiara? She hardly has the brains to manage her own money."

"Ask her if you don't believe me."

Vince had cackled, a sharp jab to Rhue's arm. Faced with

their conspiracy, Marian had disappeared in disgust for two or three days, returning when they were worn out and broke. Only once, years later, did Rhue have the courage to broach the subject with Tiara. After a New Year's celebration, one of their last, they'd made love in her private suite.

"How come your girls never leave?" he'd asked.

"Leave?"

"To marry. Or start their own business."

"They're happy here."

"But eventually they must save enough money to do something else."

"Honey, girls like them don't want nothing except three meals a day and a place to powder their noses."

"Funny definition of happiness."

"What do you know about it?" she'd asked him. "Are you happy?"

It had caught him by surprise, a personal place he didn't explore often. To avoid answering he'd turned the question around. "You're successful. You tell me."

"Success is not happiness. Success is being good at what you do, having money and power so that no one can push you around. Success is security in the brightness of daylight, but success can be lost or taken from you."

He'd waited for her to finish, his curiosity piqued.

"Happiness is different. It's pure and it stays with you forever. Happiness is security in the middle of the night." She'd risen from his side. Standing naked in the moonlight, she had refused his plea to come back to bed.

He had never known that kind of pure happiness. Even with

the horses, there was always another one to be won. Although he never told Marian she'd been right, he didn't go back to the Palace girls. Being alone suited him better.

The train whistle startled him from his reverie. The talkative woman, a widow as it turned out from her long one-sided discourse, had fallen asleep. Her head bounced against his shoulder, but she didn't wake up.

"Excuse me," the conductor said, his hand on Rhue's shoulder. "This is her stop." As if mere proximity meant Rhue was responsible for her correct departure.

He jiggled her arm. "Ithaca."

Without a word she gathered her bags and disappeared; home, he assumed, from her monologue. His wife, his ex-wife—though he rarely thought of her in those terms—would never have slept on a stranger's shoulder. Out of a sense of convention. Although Ariana'd been a strong woman, liberal in a feminist way, she'd fooled him. The unexpected pregnancy and the assumption they'd marry and live happily ever after in suburbia had caught him unaware. It had not been what they talked about while they were falling in love.

He'd felt betrayed. The plans for African explorations and Amazon summers, those dreams became poison to her. Whenever he reminded her, she grew fierce and protective of the baby inside her. She spoke less of her feelings. She insisted on a house, things in a nursery, a savings account. More and more conservative until he had to escape or be swallowed whole like the mate of a black widow spider.

In the empty train car, pulling away from Ithaca on the last straight leg to the city, he wondered if he'd made a mistake coming back. If she and Ford were still in New York, and he appeared from nowhere, begging to arrange a meeting, odds were they'd refuse. And what could he say to convince them?

Chapter Four

Ford and Evie drove for three straight hours on superhighways. They skirted towns and cities, trailed behind tractor-trailer convoys that hogged the roads. For the last hour, while Evie drove in the slow lane, she lagged behind the traffic and paid little attention to the speed limit. They had listed favorite foods and moved on to favorite books. Although they had disparate tastes, they agreed on their first choice, *The Count of Monte Cristo*. Her bloodthirsty defense of revenge amused him.

"Can I assume you have been denied a birthright?" he asked. "Or misused horribly by a lover? Or maybe punished for something you didn't do?"

"You may assume what you will, but I'll never tell." She arched the cherry red beret, another of her rainbow collection, over her forehead and gave him a fierce glance of superiority. "Torture might make me confess."

"Ah, torture," he said, "that's my kind of woman."

She honked back at a passing truck that had been stuck

behind them on a long downhill stretch. Ford laughed at her. He liked the quiet way she teased out the seriousness and found humor in small things.

"I'm starved," she said after she demolished the last licorice stick. "Woman cannot live on sugar alone."

"Sugar and grease." He held up the crumpled chip bag. "We could get off the Turnpike and try the back roads. We're almost in Paul Revere country."

"I suspected you were a history major. I haven't asked you all those personal questions, but . . . since you invited me to bury your mother . . . I probably ought to hear."

"Amherst, Class of '84. I thought you knew. Yes, history. With a minor in world peace. I did the Peace Corps for two years, caught malaria, almost died, and came home at the request of my very patient mother. Single mother, only child. That you did know."

Without comment, Evie drove on. She didn't ask about his father, though it would have been a logical follow-up question. He assumed she was digesting the new information, piecing it together with what else she knew of him. To avoid staring at her, he surveyed the countryside. The hills here in northern Connecticut were diaphanous and green. Dark chimneys peeked from the treetops, black telescopes in a sea of emerald. Like the African plains that he remembered from his overseas stint, the hills lapped into each other as far as he could see, as if the world were in fact flat and endless beyond the far horizon. In those hidden hollows were towns filled with people who gardened and painted and hiked. They attended church picnics and ski club suppers and neighborhood block parties.

He suddenly regretted the years of city life—not the time with his mother when she needed him because, without a father, it was a son's responsibility—but the blinders he'd worn about the rest of the world. It was as if he'd forgotten there was anything else. Freed from that routine, he watched the mysterious hills unfold around him and he hungered to know who lived there beneath the treetops. It would be hard to go back to his old life, the night shift, walking next to strangers, eating alone, and reading for excitement. That isolationist life didn't seem to fit with this man riding across the countryside with a woman he barely knew.

They parked in a rest stop illuminated like a prison's perimeter. When Evie spotted the official map of Massachusetts larger than life size and posted under a roofed pavilion, she streamed off. A cacophony of dogs—all shapes and sizes on leashes—rose above the road noise, even with the trucks.

"I have something to confess," he said in her ear after he caught up.

When the smallest inkling of a frown creased her forehead, he choked. Maybe she'd come because she felt sorry for him: dead mother, Spartan apartment, all those keys. Maybe he should spare her his revelations, no matter what size. While they were waiting behind an older man who had his nose on the plastic coating over the tourist attraction side of the sign, Evie elbowed Ford without turning her head.

"So? Confess."

"I don't like dogs much," Ford said. "Or cats. Animals for that matter."

She giggled. "Phew. I thought maybe you were dying of AIDS. I couldn't believe I'd gotten that big an issue wrong."

He laughed and blushed at the same time at the thought of her sitting in the borrowed apartment across the hall and analyzing his sexuality. "I'm not allergic, just not keen on the way they insist on your attention. Nose pushing, licking, barking, that kind of thing."

"It's okay by me. Actually I'm relieved. I can barely afford to feed myself. And dogs are carnivores. If there's one thing I hate, it's a pushy carnivore."

She jogged a little ways from him on the sidewalk, bent her arms to her toes, and did toe touches. In that minute of separation he saw their differences in bold print. She was energetic, young, flexible. At forty he had grown into a lifestyle somewhat dictated by his circumstances, but one he stuck to with a rigidity she wouldn't like. For all he knew, she might be a vegetarian or a Buddhist. The vehemence with which she'd agreed with him about dogs revealed a lot, but what exactly it meant for the future, he wasn't sure.

When he was with her, he felt an unfamiliar uncertainty. Life was no longer predictable. He tried to convince himself that was good, but he didn't know how well he would do if it became a constant. And yet the alternative created a huge blank chasm. Up until this point he'd lived a predictable life and what did he have to show for it?

Pop psychology told him he shouldn't replace his mother with another opinionated woman who told him what to do. But Evie didn't act like she wanted to be in charge, only that she knew what worked for her. Despite the inexperience of being young, partially unformed, she inspired an eagerness in him he'd forgotten since the feeling of Christmas Eve as a seven-year-old. Heck, if his father could jump ship at thirty-nine, Ford could, at the very least, change direction at thirty-nine.

Once the older male traveler abandoned his examination of the map and shuffled off toward the restrooms, Evie jogged back three paces to where Ford was leaning against the signpost. When she came close, he squinted against the western sky to see her better and smiled. Resting against his side, not even puffing, she tapped the logo on the map, a Puritan man above a red star.

"Sturbridge," she said, "I think that's a little town."

"We could eat burgers and keep driving."

"I love burgers."

He started to say, *I love you*, but stopped himself. That might scare her off. So far it had been too easy. His track record didn't merit this kind of easy relationship. Outside of his worries about their long-term compatibility, right now it was so comfortable he was beginning to get scared he'd blow it. And the recognition that there was something there to lose made him twice as nervous.

"I'll drive," he offered when they reached the car.

"I'll sing. My second-favorite thing." She beat him inside and was punching radio buttons, crooning snippets, totally engrossed before he backed out of the space.

"Are you going to tell me your first-favorite thing?" He asked.

"Nope. You'll figure it out." She glanced at him for a second—he felt the sharp interest and its immediate melting into something else, more resonant, more complicated. Was she trying to decide if he was worth further investigation? But she'd already moved on and was humming to the chorus of "Mustang Sally."

For now he'd have to be satisfied with her presence, a commitment of a kind, no small thing in itself that she would leave what she knew and venture off with him.

"And if I don't figure it out?"

She didn't answer because she was singing and drumming the dashboard. He forgot the confusion and wondered how she knew the words to rock songs that had been written before she was born.

Boston glowed in the distance. In a fountain of fuzzy light the peacock neon of city life rose out of the ocean, a plume of transparent colors that strained upwards with enthusiasm.

"It's a great town," Ford said, watching for the Route 128 signs. "Maybe after we take care of Mom, we should go back and do it right. Boston Gardens, Old North Church, Chinatown."

"How many times have you been here?"

"Once a year, except for the two years I spent in the Congo."

"Why once a year?"

"My mother loved the Museum of Fine Arts. Every year she brought me for their annual summer exhibition. She had an art degree from Radcliffe."

"Is that where she met your dad?"

"I don't know." The sum total of what he didn't know about his father amazed him. It hadn't seemed important until he'd realized his mother wasn't going to live forever. Now he'd never know.

Maybe they had met in Cambridge as college students. Shoulder to shoulder in the art library or at some Friday night coffeehouse, reading Brautigan, and masterminding peace rallies. If his father had been a black-armband protester when they met, the explanation for their relationship was more confusing still. Another mystery. Another gap in his own life story. He felt a little like the woodcutter's son, lost in the woods without understanding why someone who was supposed to love him had betrayed him.

A woman like Evie, though, would want to know what she was getting into up front. And he couldn't tell her because he didn't know.

By the time they wound their way through the narrow stone-edged streets of Marblehead past the third or fourth rocky beach, Ford was tired of driving. He looked forward to walking, to discovering what he had inherited from these terse New Englanders. The Cove Inn, recommended by the funeral home director who had made the long-distance burial arrangements, was a glorified motel. It perched—weathered shingles and glistening white trim—like low-tide barnacles on granite, on the highway headed north.

When he pulled in to the motel parking lot, Evie was asleep. She'd curled into his jacket, her head scrunched against the passenger door, so small she could have been a child. The discarded beret was wadded up in the crook of her elbow like a teddy bear. To wake her he pressed his hand against her shoulder. He felt the bones there, slight and fragile. A fledgling woman, she was hardly old enough to know how to be an adult, yet wiser than he in a thousand ways. She stayed asleep.

During the packing after he had rented the car, she'd suggested a single room—to save expenses—and he'd been relieved, not sure how to raise the issue. In the city they had kissed often, even fallen asleep together on his sofa watching television. Kissing, she'd announced several weeks after they met, was a vastly underrated part of a relationship. When she didn't use the word sex, he was insanely pleased. He'd grinned for an hour, until his jaw hurt and she asked what was so funny.

They'd done a stint of movie watching, searching for the perfect on-screen kiss. When he'd worked up the courage to ask how he ranked, she'd answered with a wow of a kiss. She must know that he wanted her, though he hadn't said it out like that. He was willing to let her timing control. He was willing to wait.

He gazed at the hair across her cheekbones, the bare nape, the fingers splayed in sleep, then slid away from her, shutting the door by pushing it into the frame with only a dull slur of rubber and metal meeting. He would never figure out what she saw in him. Someday, maybe someday soon, she'd get bored and drift out of his life, the way she'd drifted in: a temporary apartment, a misplaced key, the coincidental desire to travel away from the known and everyday. Story of his life. Until then he was going to do his damnedest to make her stay, even if it meant paying a detective to find out the truth about his father so there were no secrets between them.

Chapter Five

Climbing the stairs from the track to the underground terminal at Penn Station, Rhue felt his heart shift in his chest. The tightness was back. He'd stood too fast after the long hours of sitting. It was ironic. He wasn't used to so much inactivity. Other travelers pushed past him, their briefcases and bags striking him in unexpected places so that he kept thinking they were picking his pockets. Not accustomed to carrying much cash, he didn't like the feeling of constantly looking over his shoulder. Field hands fought fair, big fists and loud epithets. They didn't sneak up behind someone and pilfer what they hadn't earned.

After New York all those years ago, the first few towns he'd tried in South Dakota helped him forget the crush of traffic and the teeming sidewalks. Men outnumbered women. Children were scarce and when they did appear, they were strays. They belonged to no one. Without the confidence of family, they stayed quiet and invisible, shrinking into alleys when adults passed, turning their heads to windows. They never spoke, only sidled away from anyone who approached, not so much frightened as wary of human contact. It suited him fine.

In diners he carried on conversations with waitresses in one-syllable words and a series of wry expressions that made them laugh. He'd never been funny before. He liked to see how quickly they would shed their toughness and ask him to wait until closing. It was a game he perfected to avoid sleeping alone. Too many nights he'd woken in the middle of the night, listening for Adriana's breathing.

It hadn't taken long for him to realize the horses were more satisfying. Less demanding, yet complicated enough to hold his interest. After two winters with snow above the rooftops, he moved south. He followed the cattle herders—easy money because there weren't enough cowboys left—and discovered there were places in New Mexico where they thought New York was a foreign country. As the cattle drives and rodeos and farm jobs accumulated like blizzard snow against wire fences, he forgot he'd ever lived anywhere else. Memories, sloughed off like an old pair of shoes, were left for trash.

Despite the forty years, Penn station looked the same. The faces, blank or panicked, were all on the verge of despair. No one smiled. Knuckles on suitcase handles were white; the bones exposed like bleached cattle skulls in the desert. Lips, bloodless from being bitten, asked questions without any hope of receiving a comprehensible answer. Foreign voices, muffled in the din, jostled him. Everyone was late or lost.

When he realized he had no idea where to start looking for Adriana and Ford, he checked the duffle at Left Luggage. Once he found a hotel room and made some plans, he would come back for it. He wished he'd removed the cash, but he would have been more nervous carrying it on his person. At least it was in the deepest part of the bag. And the bag, worn threadbare in several places with two mismatched pieces of clothesline holding it together, didn't suggest riches. In a fatalistic mood he watched the man tote the bag back into the storage room. A foreigner again, Rhue'd come without plans on an undefined mission, no point in questioning the serendipity of events now.

Without the duffle he was swept up with the shifting crush toward the street. He didn't know if it was the right direction, but it didn't matter. He needed air. Because the crowd moved him along, he hardly had to make any decisions. He tried to think how long it had been since he'd ridden an escalator. On the range there was no need for escalators.

Although he was riding into the future, it carried him back to the past. Any of these men could be his son, wing-tipped, flying to a glass office fifty stories above the ground. The man two steps below elbowed past. Rhue stared. That man could be Ford.

Even if Adriana had sent a baby picture, Ford wouldn't look the same. He'd be tall and grown, in a coat and tie. Maybe he had a different kind of job. He might be an architect or a musician. He'd wear golf shirts to work or he'd sleep all morning. Adriana wouldn't have liked that, he mused, in spite of whatever praise she'd render to profess her love. In elementary school she would have encouraged her son to draw and paint. Piano lessons and a Guatemalan maid to let the boy in after school while Adriana worked late at the office. Their house would have been filled with classical music and flowering plants and shocking artwork. Only he knew what a fraud it would have been, how steeped in tradition she was that she couldn't countenance a life outside the city or windows open to rivers or waves on bare feet. Back then he'd told himself she never would have changed, he'd been right to go. But people did change. He had changed.

And yet, he'd never met another woman like her. Holding the escalator rail, he let the images rise. It had been years since he'd thought about the way her body moved, that fluid grace that made it impossible to look away. And her hair, black as the river bottom, she wore it knotted and high, a casual but elegant statement of characteristic restraint. Where an invisible strand rested exposed on her cheek, his fingers rubbed the air. But before he could, her ghost raised an ivory hand to tuck it in, leaving his own useless and inept. The feeling, familiar but long forgotten, made him wince.

At the top of the escalator the crowd moved in a great surge past the station's glass wall and out onto the sidewalk. Too fast for his bad leg. His breath sputtered. He grabbed at the person in front of him, but missed. A bench, he needed a bench, but there were none. The sidewalk was jammed with travelers and bags and uniformed attendants. Everyone talked at once. Back and forth he was jostled between rushing bodies so that he couldn't have identified north from south. He crumpled on the curb, remembering Adriana's eyes, steel gray and unforgiving, the day he'd told her he couldn't stay. His rib cage closed around his heart and he held a hand to his chest, pushing the throbbing back, inside, down.

The doctor had said, 'Rest.' He shouldn't have come back.

A fine, twittery voice spoke. "Did he hit you?"

Rhue looked into the face of a pixie, a midget girl with an old woman's skin, wrinkled but made up to highlight her cheekbones, her best feature.

"Hit me?"

"That cab." She pointed at receding taillights. "They're all mad. It looked like he knocked you off your feet."

Rhue shook his head. He hadn't even seen a cab.

"You need a drink." She spoke with more authority than he expected from such a diminutive.

"I have water in the pocket of my coat."

"That isn't the kind of drink I mean." A spidery hand rummaged next to his hip and produced the water bottle. She twisted the top and held it to his lips.

"Better?"

"Thanks."

"You don't like cities."

Although he struggled to stand, he refused her offered arm and finally righted himself on the street. A flash of yellow and a horn. She yanked him up over the curb and back to the relative safety of the sidewalk. Side by side, she was even smaller than she'd seemed at first. He bent over to hear her above the rumble of the traffic.

Her voice was like a distant flute, light and airy, sweet and mystical. "There's more time than you think. Plenty of time, you don't need to rush."

She was right, of course. How quickly he'd lost that sense of patient longevity that the prairie's open sky and forever changing horizon evoked. If a horse didn't break one day, she would the next. Or the day after. The passage of time was the only certainty. It did make him wonder. If a lifetime of training could disappear in a train ride, how significant had it been?

He massaged his arm and shoulder, swinging them to loosen the cramped muscles. As the crowd rushed around them, he stretched and twisted while the shrunken woman patted his back. The tightness faded a little.

"Walk?" she asked.

"That'd be good."

They set off. Even with the cast that made Rhue's strides jerky and uneven, the miniature woman did double steps to keep up. Just like that they were a pair. Other people on the sidewalk skirted them. To avoid the awkwardness of conversation at waist height, Rhue trained his eye on a distant spot and measured the time it took to make the mark. She chattered on, a pleasant enough stream of stories about her life and the world, half of which he missed for the din. Because they couldn't keep pace with the other pedestrians, a constant stream of people flowed around them. Many turned and glared at the logjams they caused. The open animosity of strangers pressed for time, it was something he'd forgotten about the city.

She led him away from the congestion and he let her. They passed walls of scaffold and plywood fences. Everything in this man-made world was being repaired or constructed. He'd never felt further away from what was real. It was all he could do not to turn around and get back on the train.

About the time he started to falter, she signaled a cab. She made no move to help him in, but once he was settled, they rode in silence for a dozen blocks as if she understood he needed to catch his breath. When they reached a place where the late afternoon sun filtered through trees and formed a wall of yellow haze, he recognized Central Park.

He'd forgotten the park. An oasis for city dwellers, it offered a temporary retreat from the impossible tempo of business as usual. When Adriana had realized she was losing him, she'd planned a last desperate picnic here. It had been one of their favorite places. Offering to move to the suburbs, she had let her hair down again from the formal businesswoman's bun. They had kissed with a hint of the old passion, but she was guarded, no longer willing to risk saying out loud that she loved him. And no longer sure she did, he didn't try to explain his inability to stay.

As if his tiny female guide could hear in his stifled moans the trauma of that recalled past, she let him attend to his thoughts. They stood in the elongated shadow of a skyscraper that stretched across four lanes of traffic. When he looked up, she spoke.

"Don't be sad. New Yorkers understand the value of bargaining, trading one thing for something else. The park wasn't meant for regrets, only a reminder there's more to life."

They crossed at the light and walked without talking for another ten minutes, far enough from the streets that the traffic became a soft shushing against the shore of the park, like the

ocean on a still evening. When she motioned to a bench, he
followed her orders, propping his leg on the wooden slats and
having another drink of water. The muted cries of horns and
children at play hung like a curtain in his mind. They separated
what he knew from the unreality of being here again, so close to
his past. In a place this big filled with strangers he felt more
alone than he had ever felt on the prairies. He wondered how
he had thought he would find Adriana or Ford.

"You must be a New Yorker?" he asked after she had flitted
up and down the paths to this vendor and that, gathering up
food and drinks for them.

"Actually, I've been living in Florida, but I was born about
ten blocks from here. My sister's here. She has a brain tumor.
Last Christmas they gave her two weeks. She's still fighting."

"I'm sorry," he wasn't sure whether he was apologizing for
the city or the sister or for being so slow. "I didn't catch your
name."

"Cecily Blythe."

"I'm Rhue. Rhue Hogan."

She smiled, eyeing the hotdog she'd stuck in his hand, and
nodding with her head to encourage him to eat. "Don't you just
love hotdogs?" she mumbled through a mouthful of sauerkraut
and mustard.

He took two bites, finished the hotdog, and grinned. Like a
little girl under the big tent, she cheered.

"That'll spark the old ticker."

Laughing together, they finished the fries and the coleslaw.
Between bites she filled him in on her missionary work in Florida

with the migrant workers, the sharp escalation of her sister's illness, childhood memories of the city interspersed with humorous adult confessions. Her eyes were a startling blue. The unusual hue burned from somewhere deep inside, almost hypnotizing him in its intensity. In half an hour he didn't say three words. She asked no questions, seemingly content to sit for long stretches. Periodically adding some random thought about herself or the places she'd been.

Although her mannerisms were no different from other women he'd known, her choice of words reflected a simplicity and a clarity of thought he associated with elementary school teachers and priests. Very like Marian, she created no illusions and wasn't seeking admiration. In his own eagerness to erase the guilt, Marian had been an easy friend. Because he'd elevated simplicity to a life goal, he'd taken what she'd offered without realizing that she might have needed more from him. He'd never really thought about what she needed.

Listening to Cecily speak of her life in terms of people, instead of events, caught him off guard. The underlying truth of what Cecily said—the acceptance of human relationships as the lasting value of one's life—forced him to look into the future in a way he hadn't in forty years.

Compared to her, he felt gutted and skinned like a fish, ready to go wherever the stream ran, linked to the inevitable dictates of nature. Free will, his lifeline out West, had been washed away like storm water runoff. For all that remained, it might never have existed. He was relieved Cecily hadn't asked him to characterize his own life. Under the gaze of her piercing blue eyes, things that had been so clear out west were bogged down here, like debris caught in a drain. He wasn't sure how to explain the years he'd spent away or why he'd decided to return. Although he could have apologized in a letter, he had to admit there was more to his coming than a simple apology.

Strangely enough, his distaste for the crowds and the false permanence of steel and brick faded as she talked. He was actually enjoying himself. In the hazy afternoon nothing seemed as important as simply sitting still, observing the world through her eyes. It was as if that blue filter colored the world, refreshing the weary traveler and the lonely man. Until just now with Cecily next to him, he hadn't recognized how empty his life had been.

Even Vince and Marian had kept their relationship in the present. Neither of them had asked questions or volunteered advice. Nor had he. Sitting in the middle of the teeming city, he saw his escape as an exile. Self-imposed, but an exile nonetheless.

"There, that's enough rest," Cecily said. After she flung their trash into a dented can, she took his hand and pulled him along the path deeper into the park. This time she didn't ask about his leg. Stiff and shy, he felt like a little boy being led to an initiation rite for some secret club.

"Where are you taking . . . ?"

"Shhh," she put her finger to her lips. "I want to show you something."

He was tired, but not in an unpleasant way. It was easier to follow than to strike off on his own. There was still the matter of a hotel. The duffle had to be retrieved. And sleep. He felt as if he could sleep for days. His lids hung half closed, weighted, parched. The boot, so useful on the ranch, was unforgiving on the paved pathways. His bad hip ached. Despite it being May, the city air was close and only slightly less gritty in the park.

When they arrived at a large Plexiglas wall, Cecily let go of his hand. She stood on her tiptoes and scanned the other side. Curious in spite of his building exhaustion, Rhue looked past the scratched plastic into a jungle of bushes and rocks. Beyond that, a pool glinted half-hidden by lush green. The sun made crazy squiggles of brilliance on the jade leaves.

"There," she whispered, her tone reverent.

Where she pointed an enormous lion stepped out onto the rock ledge. When the lion lifted his eyes, Rhue felt the energy from the animal flowing over and past him. The lion posed, a still life of power at equilibrium. He could have been carved from ivory or brass. He held the pose, as if announcing, after due deliberation, his own superiority. Although Rhue cleared his throat, the lion maintained his stance. In spite of himself Rhue was impressed. He stepped down from the iron bar at the foot of the Plexiglas wall.

Cecily put her hand on his arm. "No, wait." Although her head was level with his waist, she had to stretch to touch his forearm because her arms were disproportionately short. Sculptured muscles made fierce indentations in her china skin, like the marbled statues in museums. She was not like anyone he had ever known, a force unto herself.

It was hard to imagine her life outside this slice of time. Did she have a miniature house where she read half-size books and entertained other midgets? Was she married to a man like him to whom she had to yell to be heard? If she worked at a regular job, she must have custom office furniture that allowed her to reach a phone and type on a keyboard with her short arms. It amused him, though he intended no cruelty, that just when he'd begun to take his life seriously, he had a pixie for a friend.

"Patience, my friend." Cecily's fingers dug into his arm to restrain him. "Patience is the key to life."

Because she stared ahead, he did also, and so he wasn't surprised when, at the far side of the verdant undergrowth, a lioness appeared. Slinking through the tall grass she came toward the male with half-closed eyes. Her muscles slid beneath her gold coat like so many beads sinking into oil.

Wherever Adriana was, the Adriana he'd fallen in love with would have been fascinated with Cecily, a soul mate with the same sixties' astrological fervor about the meaning of life. Perhaps—he decided he was going crazy, even as he thought it—she and Adriana knew each other. Ordered their coffee at the same coffee bar, read the same books, attended the same poetry readings. The coincidence of his meeting Cecily here where he had behaved so badly years ago and her fairytale size put the whole quest in a comic mode. God was trying to tell him how absurd he was, looking for something he'd given up years ago. Ridiculous of him to think Adriana and Ford were still here, living in the same place, following the same routine, as if time had stopped while he was elsewhere.

The lioness rubbed noses with her king. Lowering herself on her front paws, she collapsed at his feet, yet hardly an obedient servant. Rhue had to admire the way she refused to concede to her mate's unconditional majesty. Without diminishing him, she was a splendid example of nature's grand plan, caged or otherwise, a reminder of purpose beyond self.

"You know," Cecily said, "They mate for life."

"Lions do?"

"They choose one partner and they only have cubs with that one. No divorces."

"Too bad they can't tell us how they manage it."

"If we wanted to know, we'd take the time to figure it out."

The urge to argue with her, to explain the explorer's desire to chart the unknown, to reconcile the craving for new experiences with the comfort of safe harbor, all these ideas surged through his brain during the split second that she, more nimble than he, cast or no cast, spun on her toes and leaped back to the path. He felt as if the conversation were unfinished.

While he was considering how to phrase his response, a man in a ragged raincoat crashed out of the bushes. He grabbed Cecily around the neck, and with his other hand covered her mouth. After an initial gasp, she closed her eyes as if meditating were a perfectly normal thing to do while being attacked by a strange man.

There was no weapon that Rhue could see. "Hey, let her–"

"Shut up." Although the man's arm tightened, his words were slurred and indistinct despite how closely the three of them stood on the path. His hair was cropped, bristled and graying. Black smudges on his cheek and forehead might have been dried blood. His eyes darted back and forth without focusing. At the tips of each finger a thick dark line marked where his fingernails were. Wavery crusted stains flowed from his wrist and down the forearm around her neck. The stale odor of endless cigarettes and worse permeated the space between them. "Shut up," the stranger repeated.

Cecily's arm rose slightly, an offhand indication of agreement, but she didn't try to speak. Rhue calculated the man's weight and height.

"Give me your money." The stranger motioned with the hand that had been over Cecily's mouth, but clapped it back immediately. "You." He nodded at Rhue, then stumbled backwards with the effort of keeping Cecily wrapped tightly enough to prevent her from slipping free.

Rhue put it all together and guessed the attacker was drunk. His arms lifted for balance, Rhue turned and swung the leg with the cast sideways. He aimed directly at the man's kneecap. When the plaster hit, the attacker crumpled. Cecily went down with him. Rhue stifled the cry of pain and grabbed at her arm. Yanking her upright and shoving her behind him, he hopped one step closer on his good leg and planted the weight of his body, cast and all, on the attacker's chest.

"What the hell kind of stunt was that?" Rhue demanded.

Buried in his raincoat, the stranger mumbled, the words garbled in grunts and groans. "Money. I need money."

Cecily adjusted her dress and restored her glasses, which were now missing a lens. She looked flustered, but she wasn't cowering or falling apart. "You could have asked."

Rhue pushed down with his heel on his prisoner. "This lady

never bothered you, never threatened to steal things from you. She doesn't deserve to be attacked."

Stooping to the fellow's eye level, Rhue slapped the rough cheek lightly to bring him back from wherever he was sinking. Vacant eyes stared back. At some point the man had drifted away from the world and lost his ability to connect to people. There was no way to know whether that explained why he robbed people.

"If you're lucky," Rhue spoke into the man's face. "They'll only charge you with assault. Seeing as no one's hurt—"

Cecily interrupted, her voice amazingly strong. "Or we'll let you go if you promise to go straight to the shelter and tell them you're ready to try rehab again." She rubbed the back of her fingers against her neck. "You won't need money for whiskey there."

The reply was barely audible.

"Did you hear the lady?" Rhue helped the man to stand.

"I'll go."

"You know where the shelter is?" Cecily asked.

When the man nodded repeatedly and shuffled off without turning around, Cecily squelched a smile.

Rhue didn't see the humor. "He could kill someone else."

She shrugged, resetting her purse on her shoulder and patting her hair back into place.

"Think he'll ever get to the shelter?" Rhue asked.

"If he hears the suggestion often enough, one day it'll strike him as exactly the right thing to do."

"What if he dies first?"

"God makes that call."

"No matter that he robs a hundred people on the way to the shelter?"

"You know the answer to that. The road to hell . . . " She motioned for him to follow. "I can forgive people. I can't change them. They have to change themselves. Look, I'll drop you on my way to the hospital. Joyce Ann'll be back from chemo and looking for me."

"Go on, don't worry about me. I can find my way."

"I wasn't worried about you. You're my hero." She laughed and pretended to salute him. "But if you decide you need me after all, call me here." She handed him a business card. The lettering was purple gothic: 'Cecily Blythe, Psychic & Marriage Counselor.' A cell number was listed along with a website address.

"Thanks again," he wiggled the toes at the end of his cast. A new soreness tingled in his shin. The single dark cowboy boot struck him as ridiculously silly next to the white plaster appendage ending in the sock. He hadn't packed the other boot because he hadn't anticipated staying.

"Anytime, night or day," she added, "But if I'm in the middle of a session, I won't answer."

Before the card was in his jacket pocket, she was striding away. When her tilted figure disappeared at the curve, he wondered if he had imagined her, fabricated the entire episode to give himself time to adjust to this place, so foreign, so different from the hollow windy plains.

On the other side of the invisible wall, without any apparent interest in the humans, the lion and lioness had rearranged themselves on the platform. He lay on his side, his head lolling over the edge of the fake stone, and she stretched out, almost touching him, with her belly exposed to the sun. Arrogant and sassy, sure of each other and their world.

Rhue wished he felt the same confidence, but the city, lurking beyond the park, took something away from him. The same way it had forty years ago. He wouldn't stay long. Find Adriana and Ford, make his peace and go, back to what he knew.

When he tried to walk, the injured leg was stiff and uncooperative. After tamping it several times on the paved sidewalk, he started back the way they'd come. Every few yards he had to stop and rest. Even in the park the open spaces were crowded; trees, bicyclers, strollers, benches, rock formations. He passed children skimming stones in the pond, lovers entwined on quilts, a bag lady feeding the ducks, and tourists whose heads were buried in their guidebooks. Although no one even glanced in his direction, he felt like a pink flamingo in a parakeet's cage.

At the park's edge he faced the street and searched for a taxi. Two policemen on horseback clip-clopped by at the corner, ten feet from where he stood. Both policemen turned to assess him. A tall man in a cowboy hat suggested someone who didn't belong, he supposed. And by deduction, different spelled dangerous. The horses' hooves tapped a sharp, look-at-me-look-at-me message on the pavement. He recognized the sound, but kept his eyes on the traffic. The very idea of horses in this teeming mass of brick and block was an incongruity too absurd to consider.

Chapter Six

*A*fter Ford checked into the motel, he went back to the car to wake Evie. It pleased him no end to think she was comfortable enough with him to fall asleep. But when he opened the car door, she was gone.

"Evie?" he called out in a panic. She could be sleepwalking, disoriented from waking in a strange place by herself. He scanned the motel lot. No Evie. When he realized the parking area opened onto the main thoroughfare, he raced through the cars. "Evie." He was yelling, his voice high and thin. It was late afternoon, but the roadway wasn't busy. He looked in both directions and across at the drive-through place. No Evie. Spinning on his heel, he sprinted back to the motel.

"Have you seen a dark-haired woman, young, petite, in the last two minutes?" He spoke loudly as he entered the lobby.

The clerk, tuned to the television, turned and frowned, but immediately returned to the show. "You came in here alone."

"After me. Maybe five minutes ago, looks kind of like a gypsy. Pretty, slight."

"I just checked you in a few minutes ago. No one's been here."

Ford threw up his hands and went back to the car. "Evie," he yelled at the top of his lungs.

She'd gone. Her first chance to escape. She realized she'd made a mistake. He was dull, unimaginative. He drove badly, distracted and careless because he wasn't used to it and because she was there in the front seat, conversing and laughing and glad to be with him. Only she'd been pretending. All along she'd been planning how to leave because she didn't want to be with him, didn't want to be driving in a car away from the friends she had and the things she knew, didn't want to be in a relationship with a loser.

He sat down in the front seat of the car where she'd been sleeping. The cushion was still warm. His long legs stuck out beyond the open door, beyond the parking space line. Holding her beret, he closed his eyes and carefully stepped into the images in his mind of how it would be with her on this journey. He winced as he breathed in the warm air trapped in the car where she had breathed in and out in that sleep of deception. One by one he packed the images of her into boxes, piled on the starched shirts and the unread Holy Bible, and closed the tops. After he sealed them with imaginary packing tape, he shoved them into the far attic of his mind.

He didn't cry. According to his mother in one of her angry monologues, his father never showed emotion. So heredity will out. But in those first minutes of grief, Ford resolved not to go back to the city. He couldn't bear to live in the apartment across from Evie's and be reminded every day of her leaving him. Or worse yet, bump into her and have to be polite as if they were strangers.

"Hey, there's a great pool. Feel like a swim?" She called from the motel office doorway with an impish grin on her face. "Funny, you don't look like a swim."

He leaped from the car and gripped her shoulders. *Don't ever do that again* is what he wanted to say. Instead he stood there speechless and gazed at her, drank her in, the twisty black hair and the moon-arched eyebrows, the lips that curved forever upwards. He couldn't speak.

"I had to go spend a penny," she said.

The restroom, of course. His body shook with relief. She'd come back.

"Diner stops serving at seven," the clerk called out from the dark interior behind her over television applause.

Ford pulled Evie into the open air, tipped his head, and kissed her, full on the lips. "Who needs earthly sustenance?"

Carrying both suitcases into the room, he left the door open and she trailed in after him. While she examined everything, he hummed an odd tune without words. He wished he could whistle. He felt that good. The curtains were avocado and the bedspread daisy yellow. On the bedside lamps, one on each side, the fringe hung brown and matted, decades old.

"Nineteen fifties," she said. "Whew. Were they repressed and trying to hide it or what?" She laughed that marvelous, gutsy laugh and flounced on one of the double beds. "This was a good idea, T. Whose idea was this?" She had taken to calling him "T" after the first Ford motorcar. "A man with a dream," she explained. When he started to debate her assertion, she'd changed the subject as if there was no point in even discussing it.

She had her clothes in the drawers and her suit on before he'd dug out his. After a glimpse of her bare back, he took his toiletries into the bathroom and laid them out on the toilet lid. His bathing suit was new, bought in anticipation of the ocean. In the city there was nowhere to swim that didn't cost more money than he made in a week. He shut the bathroom door to put it on, but felt foolish once he'd done it. After he clipped out the tags with his nail clippers, he grabbed two towels, threw back his shoulders, and went out to her.

She was at the side window, the sash thrown wide. "Come'ere," she whispered. "Aren't they cute?"

On the far side of the glistening turquoise expanse sat a wizened old man and an equally reduced woman, both in their clothes, matching white windbreakers zipped to their throats. Side by side on pool loungers, their stocking feet extended, they were both fast asleep, mouths agape. Two pairs of sturdy walking shoes—his and hers—sat between the chairs. Otherwise the pool was deserted. Ford started to squeeze Evie's shoulder, but pulled back at the last minute. He didn't want her to think he was only humoring her.

They strolled along the gravel path to the back. A long afternoon of sun had baked someone's halfhearted attempts at a garden so that the flowers stuck there were solitary and droopy. Ford put a towel on each of the first two empty chairs while Evie found two coffee cups in the trash and watered the new garden.

Sitting on the edge of the pool with his legs in the water, he watched her bend and scoop. The muscles in the backs of her legs tightened and released. It was the first time since he'd known her that she hadn't been wearing jeans.

Steadily for ten minutes she worked until the entire length of the garden soil was dark splashes of earth in erratic circles around the pinks and yellows and purples. The new leaves yearned upward toward the source of this unexpected sustenance. He knew exactly how they felt.

"You can swim without me," she said as she tipped out the last cup.

"No, I can't," he said.

"Sweet. You're so sweet, but it won't hurt my feelings. I like to lie out for a bit and get hot. Like a sauna." That quirky smile again. "I'm a creature of habit."

His turn to smile. She didn't know the half of it. After she stretched her towel on the lounger, she took off her shirt and flung it over the back rung. He worried that it might drag in the water there. While he debated whether to say something now or later, she settled into the chair, wiggling her bottom a little until she was comfortable on the plastic webbing. He could hardly keep his eyes off her.

As her body relaxed in the sun's power, she slumped. Her eyes closed. "Go ahead, really. I don't mind."

From his sitting position he kicked his feet gently. The ripples on the water spread in a fan, blue on blue, lovely, effortless. Continuing to kick he shut his eyes and waited for the urge to slide in. It would come. All his life he'd dreamed of swimming, stretching his hands into the sleek wetness, pulling and letting his body follow. At other pools some swimmers dived or jumped, but he liked to watch the ones who walked in. They entered in slow motion, savoring the silky swirls of water around them, delaying the final immersion in the otherworldly place of water. Without gravity, without solidity, they existed totally unconnected to the earth. Their faces gave away the wonder of it.

This was the shallow end. Four feet, the tile read. Starting here, his hands would pull him to the deeper water. He analyzed the slant of the painted concrete floor. He could see the drain in the deep end, not so deep really. If it didn't work, if his body plummeted, he knew he could push off the bottom with his feet. Or with his hands if necessary. He'd never been afraid of the water, just not trained to make it work for him. He knew how it was supposed to work. The scissors kick, the windmill arms, it looked easy enough. Evie was right there, not five feet from the pool. Not sleeping, listening, just soaking up the heat and the sounds. She'd hear him. If he called to her, she'd come.

He let himself slip over the concrete lip. Standing in the water, he leaned forward and sunk down shoulder high. He closed his eyes again against the sun's brightness and felt the slippery coolness silt into his body. He pulled a long swallow of air into his lungs; incense of chlorine and sun and suntan lotion all in one deep breath. With one arm in the air he bent prone to the water and dug into it. His feet swung up behind him. When he dug with the other arm, his body shot forward. He kicked his feet up and down as he'd seen other swimmers do. But when he raised his head to take a breath and opened his eyes, all he saw was water. Water rushed into his mouth, his throat, his nose, and he choked. Clawing to get to the surface, he sucked in more water. His eyes stung. His lungs burned.

"Evie," he cried, but the water drowned the words. In his panic he forgot to move his arms or kick his legs. His feet fell like a stone, and his body along with them. When his toes touched the cold slipperiness of the pool bottom, his heart stopped beating. It was not until that instant that he remembered. Bending his knees, he gave himself a tremendous push. It carried him up and up through the cold water, to the warmer water and his head crashed through to the air. Coughing and sputtering, he kicked wildly to stay afloat.

In a blur of color Evie appeared at the edge of the pool, her hand extended across the surface. "You scared me," she said. "You should have told me you didn't know how to swim."

He grabbed her hand. Hanging onto the side of the pool, he coughed and coughed. With the water inside his lungs, he couldn't talk. The rushing sound of rising through the water filled his head.

"Sorry," he managed finally.

"I'm not clairvoyant, you know. I can't guess these things. You said you loved the ocean. How was I supposed to know?" She rattled on, pushing the hair off his face with her fingers and pounding his back until he stopped sputtering. "I'll hate it if you hide things from me. I'm not good at secrets."

Once she stopped talking, he pulled himself out of the pool. They sat side by side on the warm concrete.

"You're crying," he said.

"Am not."

"But Evie . . ."

"I'm not."

"Okay. Whatever you say."

He used the towel to dry off his head and arms. Without taking his eyes off her, he lay down on the lounge chair. What he wanted was for her to come and lie next to him, but she stayed by the pool edge, her face turned away. Beside her was a puddle of water where he'd been. Her fingers patted the puddle. With her index finger, she drew patterns on the stippled concrete. They stayed separate like that for a long time.

The old couple awakened, murmured to each other, heads together. They rose stiffly and walked, hand in hand, past the garden, enveloped in shadows now, to the far end of the motel. Ford tried to make out their words, but they weren't real words, just feelings that passed between the two of them like a breeze, warm and cooler, thick and spare, a connection he could almost see. When they had gone, he projected his voice to where Evie sat.

"Will you teach me?"

They missed the diner and had to drive into the little town to find something to eat. After clam rolls and iced coffee, they walked the main street. Evie ogled the stainless steel gardening tools in the hardware store window and Ford admired the circular bandstand in the center of the park. They passed several families.

"Good evening," one father said with a polite nod to acknowledge them. A baby gurgled from the stroller. The mother pushed steadily behind him.

"Norman Rockwell, where are you?" Evie said after the couple's other two children had raced around them in circles, then reeled off like fishing line on the fly. Brother and sister shrieked at their parents to wait up. Ford thought about taking her hand.

At the curb they waited side by side, despite the absence of cars, for the neon walking man figure to appear. The streetlights stopped after the third storefront, leaving the road out of town unlit and murky.

"You haven't asked me about my family," she said into the night, which accompanied them now like a noonday shadow.

His brain spun fast. "You told me about your sister."

"Just that she lived in the city."

"Well, she must work days, because you had to say good-bye to her at night. And she doesn't have kids, because you never mention nieces or nephews. It's your business what you want to tell me."

She drew apart. It broke the pattern of their feet hitting the pavement in unison. He could no longer feel the air between them weaving in and out of her limbs and his. When she shivered, he swore to himself. He'd only meant to show her he cared enough to let her tell it in her own way. If he tried to explain, he would bungle that too. Especially when he wanted to know it all, every little detail about her, her first word, her memories of Christmas, whether she prayed out loud or telepathically, what she read on rainy Sundays, whom she admired most.

It was a curse, his well-intentioned caution about asking for more. He began to count the string of friends, male and female, whom he had discouraged by giving them too much space.

Like museum guards, watchful but unwilling to meet your eyes, he and Evie ambled along the narrow sidewalks. Cooler evening air settled itself into the town all around them. Where the houses ended and the beach railings appeared, they turned and without consultation strolled back on the other side of the street. He could feel himself, mired in depression and uncertainty, slow down and drag his heels on the uneven pavement. The struggle to begin again consumed him. A new subject, untainted, easy and affectionate without being pushy, the challenge preoccupied him until he realized the rental car was right around the corner and he'd missed his chance.

At the last intersection she hooked her arm in his. "Is there supposed to be a moon tonight?"

Her forgiveness poured over him like summer rain, steamy and thick from a sudden thunderstorm. With a squeeze of his elbow, he pinned her hand to his side, wanting her to feel his appreciation for the restored connection.

"We can check the weather report in the paper. It's back at the room."

"Our room," she said.

"Say that again."

That first night they slept in separate beds. It was an accident he didn't know how to explain, as eager as he was to make love to her. While she was in the bathroom, presumably brushing and flossing and such, he folded back the covers and put the lilac blossom he'd picked outside on her pillow. He started to climb in the other side and then decided that would be rude. How did he know which side she liked? He didn't dare presume this leap in their relationship.

He tried waiting in the chair, but it faced the bathroom door. Too weird to hover, as if he were waiting to pounce on her. Nervous to the point of restlessness, he paced the tiny room. He memorized the wallpaper stains. In the mirror—framed in two-toned plastic, nailed to the wall—he recognized panic in his eyes. He counted the number of times she turned the water on and off. Maybe she was avoiding him. Or nervous too. But when he checked his watch, it had only been four minutes. Finally, he switched on the television and stretched out on the extra bed, what he'd come to think of as the extra bed.

The newscaster whizzed through his report. He quoted the president, with emphasis. Things were heating up in several African countries. They were debating whether to send troops to keep the peace. What peace? Had there ever been a time when humans farmed and ran factories and loaded ships without fighting about something? Even in prosperous countries an individual man coveted what his neighbor had. Or his boss. Sometimes even his brother.

Surely that was worth a smidgeon of gratitude for his father. At least he hadn't left two sons to bicker over who took better care of their mother or who would inherit the silver candlesticks.

Ford's head sank into the too-soft pillows. The television droned. He closed his eyes and drifted into a reverie where memories mixed with fantasy. A passel of children played with him in his Long Island yard. His mother wore a flowered apron— something she'd never done in real life—and served warm cookies to the whole crew. His father, in one of those starched dress shirts, his tie loosened, appeared in the kitchen window. Home, he announced through the open window. Appearing at the screen door, he shrugged off the suit coat as his wife left the children to kiss him hello.

When Ford woke up, it was morning. Evie had covered him with her bedspread and slept by herself. The lilac blossom sprouted from a glass of water on the bedside table between the two beds, like a misplaced purple bedroom slipper. He couldn't help laughing, which woke her.

"I slept like a pig after a mud slide," she said.

"And you feel good?"

"I feel great." She fluffed the pillow and laid her head sideways, looking right at him across the divide between the two beds. "T?"

"Uh-huh?"

"Did you dream?"

"Oooooh, that's a risky question to ask when you've just shared a motel room with a guy." The possibility that she guessed he'd been dreaming was a little too coincidental. He wasn't used to someone knowing him that well. If she knew that, she might know when he was worried or scared even before he was ready to talk about it.

"No, seriously, I'm doing a little research."

"That sounds even worse."

"T."

"Okay." He stretched one hand across and touched her bare arm outside the covers. He let his fingers rest on her warm skin.

"I didn't dream last night. Too tired from all those laps you made me do."

Although she didn't push for more, he could tell she was disappointed. He'd let her down somehow and he wasn't at all sure why he had lied except to have his father appear suddenly in a dream might take some explaining.

"But I do dream a lot," he added before the silence became awkward. "Mostly about the ocean. It's a recurring dream though. Does that count?"

"Are you swimming in the dream?"

"No, I'm dreaming."

"You're stalling."

So she had recognized the deceit. That was a good sign. She wanted the truth. He would have to confess or risk hurting her over not sharing. He sat up, swung his feet to the floor, and hunched over, elbows on knees, closer to her head on the pillow. Even fresh from sleep she looked alert and focused. For an instant he felt flattered, but he told himself it was her nature, curious and impatient.

Were they too different? He tried to think of all the couples he knew who had been together a long time. There weren't that many. Evie propped herself on her elbow, a gesture he took as encouragement.

"Having trouble remembering?" she asked.

"Oh, no. The ocean is always there, but it's not real. It's as if there is no far side, no rest of the world, just a curtain painted to look like waves and sky. Something ought to be there and it haunts me."

"So what happens?"

"All right, already, give me a chance. I don't think as fast as you."

She buried her face in her pillow and reappeared with a guilty grin.

"It starts with a small boat just over the crest of the last wave. I'm waiting on the beach. I can't see myself, but I'm definitely there, because people stop and talk to me." He had to force himself not to lean over and kiss her. When she smiled as if she knew what he was thinking, he looked away. "The boat floats away, though. It doesn't ride the waves in like I expect it to. And while I'm busy trying to figure out who's in it and why they're headed out instead of in, a person—a faceless person—starts down the beach toward me from the rocks or the houses."

"It's always the same?"

"There aren't always houses in the distance. Although when there are, they are spectacular geometric shapes with angles and brilliant tropical colors. Not at all like actual houses."

Evie's eyes were closed. She must be concentrating. With extraordinary restraint, he kept his hands from touching her face and continued his description.

"I forget the boat because I'm so busy watching the person until he's close enough to speak to me. Usually the face stays out of focus, even when he speaks. I never answer his questions, and sometimes he's angry at me."

"It's a fearful dream?"

"More anxious. I worry. That he'll walk right past. Or I won't be able to answer the questions I know are coming."

"Who do you think it is? The man in the dream?"

"Me, maybe. You know, my subconscious self."

"Some person in your life you wanted to impress."

He shook his head. "It's curious, though. Even while he makes me nervous, I don't question his right to ask."

"Do you do anything in the dream besides wait?"

"If I stay asleep long enough, I try to walk out to the boat to get away from him."

"You do swim."

"No, I sink."

At her gasp he reached over and touched her lips with his fingers. "Maybe now I won't."

Chapter Seven

*R*hue stood in the phone booth with the door open for air, the leg in the cast wedged against the folding door so he had both hands free for the phone. His whole body felt revved up—his heart rate, his pulse, and his temperature—like someone had stoked the stove. When he tried wiping his face with his sleeve, his hand knocked the glass wall. His knuckles throbbed. He cursed.

"Well, really." A coiffed woman in a business suit blurted as she passed, her heels clicking her distress on the pavement. She was gone before he could apologize.

The city phonebook—the cover missing and the yellow pages torn in half the way only a full-blown Hollywood gorilla could have done—showed eighteen entries for F. Hogan. Good thing it wasn't Boston or the turn of the century when Irishmen had flooded the cities. There was no Adriana Hogan or even A. Hogan, though Rhue doubted she would have kept his name no matter how awkward it would have been to explain at every school function and church social a son with a different last name. He folded down the page with A. Simmons, her maiden name, and turned back to H.

After he lined up quarters on the shelf, he began dialing Hogans. The first seven were female according to their answering machines. No point in leaving a message. Even if one were Ford's wife, they couldn't call him back.

Before he'd found the payphone, he'd wandered for a bit, surprised that he remembered the order of the streets. It amazed him how many events came back to him. The night they'd walked home from the theater, fifty-odd blocks, holding hands and quizzing each other on history trivia. The marathon antiwar concert in the park when Adriana, passionate about the audacity of Americans to interfere in someone else's business, had handed out leaflets and debated with passersby. They'd both been freshly graduated PhD's, insistent that the world was badly organized, but fixable.

The irony struck him now, forty years too late. How eager they'd been to meet the world head on. How important it had seemed to change the future. And then he'd run away, changing his own future, but hers too. Except at the time he'd told himself she was the one giving up on their dreams.

In spite of the confusing memories, the walk from Central Park had given him time to plan. To burst in on an abandoned wife and son required more preparation than he'd allowed in his precipitous flight from the doctor's admonitions. The accident had propelled him into action before he could think it through. He should've telephoned from Montana. That way Adriana and

Ford would have time to recover from the shock of his phone call. If he'd found a hotel room first, they could call back when they were ready to talk. Perhaps they'd confer and plan together what to say to him. He decided to call Ford first. That would mean someone Adriana trusted would break the news to her, preferable to his telephoning her directly and making her mad all over again.

He played out the scenario in his mind as he'd done so routinely with the horses. Once the meeting was arranged, he could swing by the train station for his duffle. He'd have to traverse the escalator and the crowded station again. He hadn't asked how long luggage check would keep his bag, but the longer it was left, the more tempting it might be to the handlers.

Although taxis sped by one after the other, by the time he could see they were empty, there was not time to maneuver the cast to a place where they would see his signal. Standing in the street was too risky. Not quite rush hour, as the cars skated past the red lights, he sensed the edge of that remembered five o'clock panic. Caught up in the anxiety and indecision, he'd opted on the spur of the moment to check the phone listings.

In the narrow airless booth the cast bit into his ankle. With his finger he probed a large raw place at the top edge of the plaster. The ugly blister had burst. He wedged a leftover paper napkin there, but it hurt either way. A slow dribbling moan accompanied his standing on a broken leg with the heavy phone book balanced against his hip. Between the last ring and the pickup at the other end of the line for each telephone call, he choked back the pain. If a real voice answered, he planned to drop the book. The conversation would be dramatic enough without the moan.

After the tenth call, a busy signal, the book fell by itself. In an awkward attempt to retrieve it, he lost his balance and crashed down against the hinged door of the phone booth. His good leg twisted and he ended up on the ground, knotted in a way that made rising on his own almost impossible. Several passersby stopped long enough to register his predicament—from a safe distance—but no one rushed over to help. Small drops of blood spotted the cast. He must have cut something. Although the gash had to be on his face, he resisted the urge to feel it with his dirty hands.

The sense of well-being he'd gained from Cecily's quirky optimism dimmed. He might fail. For forty years he'd prided himself on setting a goal and meeting it. This was different because he had so little control. It wasn't all up to him. His success depended on other people, people he didn't know, who already categorized him as unreliable, at best.

As he lay propped against the phone booth pondering how right the decision to return seemed just a few days ago, it struck him that he must have ridden the mare. If he'd collapsed by the river before mounting, no one would have found him in time to transport him to the hospital. He'd be dead. He must have taken Delilah back over the ridge and closer to the ranch. Or she'd taken him.

It was probably Clark's kid who'd found him. Ironic, the punk ranch hand who knew everything and nothing, who considered him an interfering old man. Perhaps he'd driven back to be sure Rhue wasn't bothering the horses. He felt nauseous at the idea of the boy discovering him on the ground, unconscious. Seventy-nine wasn't old enough not to be vain.

Still the discovery that he'd ridden Delilah reassured him. He wasn't helpless. If the fall hadn't stopped him, the challenge of finding his lost family wasn't going to either. He wasn't ready to join Vince yet.

While he was still contemplating how best to resume standing in the narrow space, two young men with baggy pants and scraggly facial hair—it didn't justify the word beard—tripped over his legs. At the unexpected pain he cursed before he could stop himself. The bigger of the two fellows caught the door handle and, with an amazing gymnastic pirouette, righted himself. The other one was so deep in conversation that he plowed into the back of his associate at full steam. The expletives were no different here.

After squaring off and throwing several amateur punches at each other, the two kids—for they weren't men as he'd thought at first—scrabbled into a wrestling stance. Arms grappling shoulders, they continued to curse at each other despite the obvious standoff. The sidewalk was suddenly deserted. Rhue registered two pairs of combat boots. At one waist he saw a flash of silver.

Here was danger. Unprepared, he was unable to free himself. Wedged inside the mechanical door, his body throbbed in a dozen places. If these punks looked closely enough, they'd find the moneybag in his cast. And the luggage check receipt in his pocket. Once they'd taken his money he'd never convince a taxi to take him anywhere. And asking Adriana or Ford to ante up was unthinkable.

Rhue mustered his best authoritative voice. "Hey, hey, hey."

After shoving his companion away, the older boy leaned down and stared, inches from Rhue's unshaven face. The boy jerked his head backward. From out of the dreadlocks, a face appeared. Despite the matted peroxide tangle, which suggested more vanity than vigor, belligerence oozed from every limb.

"It's a free country," the other boy yelled.

Before Rhue could respond, the first kid yanked the other one back. "Cut it out," he said to his friend. He reached down, thrust his hands under Rhue's armpits, and pulled him to upright as if he were straightening a trash pile. "Sorry, fella, not a good place to run out of hooch. You okay?"

The second fellow had backed off. He avoided Rhue's legs with the deliberate placement of the serious boots. From several feet away, he railed. "Jeez, Wizard, leave the guy alone. He might not want to get up. He has just as much right to sit there as you do to walk where you want." They seemed to have forgotten their earlier dispute.

"F-you, Rip, he doesn't look so good." And to Rhue in a more controlled tone, "Are you feeling alright, buddy? You look a little puckish."

It was such a grandmotherly word that Rhue laughed, a full, sudden appreciation for the joke, even if it was a joke on him. After a lifetime of adventures, it was ludicrous to be brought low by a phone booth. The two boys eyed him suspiciously for a second, but when he continued to shake with laughter, they joined in. As other people came along and saw the three of them hacking away on the street corner, they sidestepped the trio. The boys and Rhue laughed all the harder.

"Man, that's some good stuff you been drinking," Wizard said. He chuckled again, losing control and bellowing with laughter. "Got any more?"

Rip—if Rhue had heard the name correctly—made a pantomime of searching for a bottle. The boy circled in place until he had to grab the handle of the phone booth himself to keep from falling with dizziness. People slowed to stare, but kept their distance.

"Enough of that." Wizard shushed his friend with a flapping arm. "Last thing we need is cops." He put a hand under Rhue's elbow to steady him and leaned close to his head as if he thought Rhue might be hard of hearing. "Seriously, man, you don't look like you've eaten for days. Do you have a place to go?"

Before Rhue could think which answer was safest, Wizard took one of Rhue's arms and Rip, the other. Pinned in between with no way to escape, Rhue panicked. They might have misinterpreted his silence as an indication of homelessness. Now that they knew he was helpless and alone, they meant to drag him somewhere and take what they could.

"Wait," Rhue choked out in half-breaths. "The phone . . ."

Wizard patted his stomach in pantomime. "Dinner first." Unrelenting, he tightened his grip on Rhue's arm.

After four or five uneven steps, Rip leaned down and analyzed the cast. "Nice boot," he said and the boys broke into guffaws again.

Limping along for half a block on the main thoroughfare, they turned the corner into a dead-end alley and pulled Rhue up short by two dumpsters. He tensed. This was the perfect place to knock him out and strip him clean. No one would see. While the boys moved away a short distance to confer, Rhue kept one eye on them and the other on the open end of the alley. Wedged against the wall and one of the dumpsters, he tried to summon enough energy to run. The cast felt like stone. His mind wouldn't connect to his feet. He didn't think he could move fast enough to get past them and back to the busier sidewalk. Relying on other pedestrians to defend him didn't make sense either as hostile as these New Yorkers had acted so far.

When Rip raised his voice, Wizard gestured with his hands. The argument intensified. Rhue wiped his forehead with his sleeve and wished he'd objected more strongly to leaving the phone booth when there were witnesses who might have stepped in to save him. Although there'd been nights when some drunk cattle hand had tried to roll him, he'd been more fit and without the awkward cast. When you knew a place, you knew what to avoid, when to put up your guard. Since Vince's death, he'd stopped paying attention. This fatalism was new to him. And with the recognition that he had nothing worth protecting, he realized how much of his life he'd spent searching. For what? The answer eluded him.

Whatever he'd come back here for, he wouldn't find it face down in the dumpster. He edged toward the metal fire escape, judging the distance he'd need to swing the cast against them if they attacked.

The boys' angry voices, which had filled the alley, sank into mutters. After shaking his fist at Rip, Wizard lit a cigarette and chucked the wrapper in the corner. The other boy sulked. He jammed his hands in his pockets as if he were damned if he'd concede to his friend in even as small a way as smoking. The wispy cloud from the one cigarette dawdled above their heads, eventually floating high enough to get lost in the small window of sky between the buildings. Although Rhue's shoulders ached from the tension, he didn't dare sit down on the metal steps and give them the advantage of height as well.

A thunderclap made all three of them stare upward. Just as the last edge of blue sky slipped behind the roof, the first fat drops smacked the pavement.

"Okay, Cowboy Man, time to go." Wizard shot his cigarette butt at the ground and twisted his heel on it before commandeering Rhue's arm again.

When Rip's hand started to come out of his pocket, Rhue, expecting a knife, struggled to slip free. Wizard tugged back.

"Come on, come on," he nodded at Rip and together they pulled the cowboy into the dark end of the alley. Rhue struggled to come up with an argument that might dissuade them.

As they tugged him between them, Rhue could see that the door in the far wall was staved open with a chunk of newspaper. A gaping hole glared from the metal where the handle should have been; the hole's edges raw and sharp as if a giant had single-handedly ripped off the knob. Rhue tried to turn around, but they kept pulling him further into the narrow hallway.

"You don't wanna go back out there, man. It's pouring."

To see their expressions and whether they were serious, Rhue had to crane his head. They looked straight enough. Inside, past the clutter of discarded boxes, Wizard opened a second door. Facing the street was a tiny cafeteria, its metal tables jammed together between a wall of windows and a double shelf of stainless heating trays. Rhue spun around in search of a way out. Many of the tables were already taken. Mostly single men hunkered down over trays of food. It looked busy enough for temporary safety. At least he could sit down and figure out what to do from there without worrying about a knife in his gut.

One of the kerchiefed waiters behind the counter yelled over the general hum of kitchen noise. "Yo, Ripper, your mama's been here."

"What'd you tell her?"

The waiter shrugged. "What I always say. No thank you. She's your Mama."

Rip leaped at the waiter across the counter, sending paper cups in a shower around them. At the commotion, a bald man in a stained apron rushed from the kitchen, arms flying. "Hey. Scumbags. I don't want no trouble in my place." Separating them, he glared at Rip who was edging away.

"Ignore Leo," Wizard muttered at Rhue, elbowing him into line as he ducked his head in the cook's direction. The boy shot one of the cafeteria trays along the metal rack toward Rhue and took one for himself. "He's got ulcers."

The cook stepped toward Wizard. "What you say, boy? You talk bad about Leo after I feed you, let you work for food, don't rat you out to the truant officer?" Leo gestured for the waiter to get back to work.

"No, sir. I was telling my friend here how hard you work even though you're sick with those ulcers."

"Okay, okay," Leo pointed at Rip and grinned. "I forgive him, but no more fighting. And no free meal today." After Leo disappeared behind the swinging doors, Wizard motioned for Rip to choose his dinner. At the register when the boys pulled loose dollars and coins from their pockets and began to count, Rhue realized how young they really were. No wallets, coins mixed in with scraps of paper and subway tokens. Lunch money squirreled away? Or change pilfered from soda machines?

He thought of Cecily and her generosity with lunch. While psychic powers didn't impress him, she had sensed his dilemma somehow. The boys were too busy with problems of their own. If they'd meant to rob him, they would've taken the opportunity in the alley and not made a public display of being seen with him. There must be something else. Maybe they were bored, eager for something different than the everyday.

The cashier, though, frowned at the delay. When her Spanish curses had no effect on the boys, she smiled at Rhue over their heads in apology. Back and forth the two friends spat words at each other so fast Rhue couldn't follow it all. It might have gone on forever—Marx and the capitalist machine were mentioned— but after he pulled a one hundred dollar bill from the cast, they fell silent.

When Rip bent to look at the magical leg, Wizard whacked him on the head. "Pervert."

Reaching back for a second dessert, Rip shrugged. "Thanks, old man."

With a huge grin at the cashier, Wizard ushered him off to a window table.

Although the boys ate with enthusiasm, they continued to bicker. Rhue had time to analyze possible escape routes.

Across the alleyway graffiti symbols, drawn with paint and chalk, covered the concrete walls. Obscured by sheets of rain that slapped against the window like a spontaneous rock-and-roll riff, the indecipherable letters appeared and disappeared; clear one minute and blurry the next. The storm crashed overhead. Rain ran down the walls in ragged torrents. Riding through the Montana foothills, herding cattle, he'd been chased by the same weighty sense of each man's isolation. Whatever you'd said or done, mean or generous, joyous or tragic, melted into the soil like the rain. History was merely the fact of your own past. In the end there was only you in the present, what you said or did that day.

Vince had gone to ground with a scattered handful of friends to watch his final descent, but what was left of him now? His friends, the ones who remembered, would die soon. Within a matter of years the space he'd occupied would be filled with new faces and new adventures. This weariness with the world, Rhue knew, was an old man's burden. When he'd left Montana, he'd been hopeful, almost eager that there might be something more. Sitting here, surrounded by strangers, he had to wonder if there was something different about dying if you left a child behind. Wasn't a child a contribution to the future, something created, a story with an unknown resolution?

Gravy congealed on his plate while he watched the rain and tried to figure out a plan. Although he was used to mediocre food, he was having trouble swallowing the cafeteria selections. Perhaps Marian had felt this way when she first got sick, distracted and not a little paranoid. If she had recognized the finiteness of life before she lost the connection to the everyday, did that explain why she'd let the rest go? He forced himself to dig into the potatoes, no point in adding to his disorientation by being weak from hunger.

"So, big man, where you from?" Rip asked. "It's pretty obvious you're not city."

"Montana," Rhue offered, surprised at the truth. He'd grown accustomed to saying around. Rarely did he volunteer personal information. He couldn't remember the last time he'd talked to strangers, much less three in one day. It was hardly a conversation though.

Eating avidly, Wizard didn't look up at all. As Rip picked at what remained of his food, he made no effort to hide his examination of the man from Montana.

"Born there?" he asked.

"No."

"Me neither." Clowning, the boy thumped his own chest. "Florida. My ma's an army brat. Had me early and left home right after for the Big Apple. She likes all the wacky people here, says it reminds her of the circus."

Rhue wasn't sure he wanted to hear more. He nodded at Wizard.

"I'm in between places. Dad's a hard ass, but I bug him, know what I mean? He might be better now. I've been gone a while."

"Hah." Rip forked a potato. After he jammed it into his mouth, he waved the empty fork in the air at his friend. "You don't believe that."

"Mind your own GD business."

Nodding to one and then the other, Rhue felt a little like a Kewpie doll in the rear window. "Thanks for . . ." he wasn't sure how to characterize what he now considered to be a rescue. He could see himself frozen in the rainy phone booth; the cast disintegrating as he sat shivering, pinned on the ground. Suddenly the idea of talking on the telephone to Ford after all these years struck him as idiotic. If he'd been Ford, he would have hung up on anyone who claimed to be his father, the father who'd walked away.

The physical reality of being a parent was no different than the physical reality of being black or male. There was no talent in being born into it. To make a go of fatherhood, you had to work at it. And if you botched it up, you had to make up the lost ground, the same way you worked a colt until he took the bridle. If you were serious about turning things around.

When he looked up from his reverie, the boys were waiting for him to finish his sentence. "Thanks for stopping. I don't know how I would have extricated myself."

"No problem," they mumbled, glancing around the restaurant and at each other. Perhaps they didn't have much experience with gratitude.

After a blank moment where the three of them stared at each other, Wizard winked. "A stuck pig, isn't that what they say where you're from?"

Rip ignored him and stuffed the trash into his milk carton. Rhue hadn't meant to put him on the defensive with the ten-dollar word. He felt a little like a circus performer on the high wire, balancing, ever balancing between his own needs and the boys'. With Vince and Marian he hadn't paid enough attention, but he could see that the friendship he'd prized so for its independence had been limited by boundaries he'd set. He hadn't wanted to answer questions and so he hadn't asked any. It was like standing at the ridge of the Grand Canyon and not looking over the rim. Only here, years after the fact, in this crazy world of disconnect and randomness with its fleeting splices of intimacy did he realize he might have missed something important.

When all the food was gone except for a jiggling half of Wizard's chocolate cream pie, Rhue decided he would trust them with his search. His other options were shrinking with the daylight. Pushing the tray aside, he swept the Formica with the side of his palm, an old habit before shuffling cards on the ranch house table.

"I'm looking for two people."

Rip and Wizard exchanged glances. "To do what?" They said in unison.

"No, not like that. Specific people I haven't kept up with in . . ." he hesitated, unsure how to describe the story of his life in ten words or less, "My ex-wife and my kid." It sounded so cold and unfeeling as if they were baseball players he'd lost track of, trades and seasons ago.

Rip shoved the chair back from the table in a loud squeal of outrage. "Man, we take up for you, pick you up and cart you over here, eat with you, and you're just another dumb jerk like my old man."

Wizard interrupted. "Cool it. You don't know that. He could have reasons. Anyway the man just paid for your food. You oughta be thanking him."

Rip sat down, his head lowered. He shoved the tray from hand to hand to make it clear that no reason could possibly be good enough.

Wizard knocked the back of Rip's head with his hand. "Hey, are you perfect?"

"Jeez," was all Rip said.

Wizard took a huge gulp of his watered-down Coke, swallowed it whole, and turned back to Rhue. "This wife and kid, they still live in the city?"

Rhue shrugged his shoulders, oddly grateful not to have to explain the leaving and the years of separation. "That's why I started with the phonebook."

"You came all the way from Montana without knowing whether they even live here?"

As absurd as it sounded, his reasons wouldn't sound too much clearer. To the backdrop of fading thunder, he saw there was no escape. They were waiting. They wanted to know more. Although Cecily hadn't pried—an adult understanding of regrets and desires—if he was going to ask the boys to help, they would require an explanation. They deserved it.

"My wife and I planned to travel, Peace Corps or something like that, Africa, India. We were saving to go. Then she got pregnant. It wasn't the deal we made. So I left."

"How d'you know she had a son?"

"I called once and she told me."

Rip's fork dropped onto his plate with a startling clatter. "Man, I wouldn't have told you a damn thing."

In the uncomfortable silence Rhue accepted their disgust as his due. Tens of hundreds of times since he'd turned away from Adriana that afternoon in the park he'd thought the same thing, but shoved it back into his subconscious. Because she hadn't cried, he convinced himself she was glad he was going. More likely she hadn't cried because she hadn't wanted him to know how much it hurt. He'd forced her into sharing his dishonesty when it wasn't her nature. If he'd done that to the horses, their disrespect for him would have translated into failure as a trainer. If he'd done that to Delilah, pretended they were old friends, she never would have let him mount.

Rip knocked his tray against Rhue's to get his attention. "You think your old lady still loves you?"

"That's not why I came."

Wizard held his drink halfway to his mouth as if he were stunned by the idea of someone admitting he was the one at fault after all that time. "Why did you come?"

While Rhue's mind scrambled, he worked his fingers into the cast and repositioned the napkin on the blister. He rubbed the muscles in his thigh. He needed sleep. His brain chugged at a crawl, unable to stay focused on any idea except the image of being prone and freedom from the unforgiving plaster. "There are things I need to say. If my father had left me, I think I'd like to hear them. Maybe, maybe not."

Rip banged at Wizard's sleeve, like a drummer building toward a riff, but Wizard ignored him.

"What kind of work they do?" Wizard kept his eyes on Rhue.

"She used to run an art gallery."

Rip continued to hit Wizard's arm. Wizard frowned at his friend and raised his voice. "What?"

"There's that locator thingy on the Internet. You put in the name and it tells you all about the person. Address, job, awards, you know."

"Yeah, Google."

Rhue laughed, but they didn't. They were serious.

"It's an awesome search engine," Rip explained.

In Rhue's imagination the fiery engine of a gigantic silver train with brilliant bulging headlights blanched the terrain. Each rock, rail, and bush became vividly pinpointed against the sandy hillside. In the sweeping lights figures scurried on magical train platforms. Surreal faces without limbs, illuminated in the dusty backdrop, moved across craggy hillsides, scrub pine, and tumbleweed. Montana was still there, in the back of his mind, a lifetime of Montana.

"A search engine on the computer," Rip added.

The kid's gloating was understandable. Although Rhue had sidestepped the computer age, he understood enough to know that whatever they were talking about, he didn't know how any of it worked. It was part of the next generation's world, not his.

"How old are you anyway, Pops?" Rip asked without waiting for an answer. "A search engine is like a modern-day encyclopedia. 'Cept that it changes every second, with each new piece of information. All you need," he paused like a magician before he produced the rabbit, "is the full name of the person you're looking for."

Tipping his hat off his forehead in a gesture of impatience, Wizard held up his palm to stop Rip from speaking. Without the hat, an angry scar on his temple was exposed. Although Rhue knew he was staring, he couldn't look away. The scar added to the boy's haunted look. The way he'd glared at Rip would have sent a lot of kids running. The whole thing might still be a scam. While Rhue knew next to nothing about the two, they'd seen that he had a handful of cash at his fingertips. To kids with pennies in their pockets, the change from a one hundred dollar bill would seem like a fortune.

Even if they were being straight with him, no con, asking for help from anyone felt uncomfortable after he'd managed for himself so long. But he was stuck. The raw place on his leg stung and the storm rattled all around them. There wasn't much he could do on his own.

"Adriana and Ford Hogan," he announced, hoping the names would be enough.

Rip's chair shot away from the table in one long scrape. "Piece of cake."

Wizard rose also. With one efficient movement he brushed all the trash onto one tray and stacked the other two underneath. He was halfway to the trash can before Rhue even understood they were leaving.

"C'mon, man," Rip called back. Hands in their pockets, the two boys huddled on the sidewalk. Their shoulders sagged—

talking or not, Rhue couldn't be certain—while they waited in the mist for him to clunk around the Formica tables with the plaster leg.

The chance for escape was here, but it was no longer an option. He'd made another split-second choice. Like leaving the hospital, the alternative of looking for Adriana on his own held no appeal.

"Where are we going?" he asked once he opened the door, but the boys simply started walking, more eager than he. They stayed half a block ahead of him. Sour smells from the gutter puddles reminded him of the thief in the park. His stomach churned. He'd eaten too much. His head, hot and heavy, pounded behind his eyes. The air, which should have been cooler after the storm, draped about him, smothering and oppressive. The most pleasant thing he could think of was a nap and he had nowhere to take one.

He would have liked to rest in a quiet place, to think out a strategy for talking to Adriana and Ford, the kind of campfire planning he and Vince and Marian had done a thousand times until it felt like second nature. But alone in a hotel room, he wouldn't have discovered the boys and the computer link. Already he felt closer, just for talking about it. Saying the names out loud made Ford real somehow. The lost baby boy traded for a man with a face and a job. It made the absence of open sky bearable.

At the traffic lights they all stood together. Cars whizzed around the corner. As Rhue listened to their conversation, he forgot all about asking them where they were headed or how much further it was. Excited about their spontaneous mission, they traded stories about computer games and programs. So fast did the unfamiliar terms fly that Rhue felt like a time traveler. Although he'd never before considered himself an uneducated man, the boys spoke a language as foreign to him as Japanese. Despite his Yale degree—in this city, at least in the world he had abandoned, an Ivy League education summoned a currency of respect—he'd grown out of the habit of solving cerebral puzzles.

Out West a college degree was a liability. No one asked about your past, because everyone had something to hide. The only thing that mattered was the day immediately before you; whether the cattle were delivered on time, whether the mares foaled, whether the rope hit the mark. For forty years production defined his value. His mind? No one even paid attention. Where he'd been living, there was enough space for everyone as long as you understood your reputation depended on how efficiently you used that space. It had suited him to live like that, without needing anyone to support or promote.

In the city it was different. Everything was connected. If the garbage collector failed to show up for work, the streets jammed. Taxis couldn't deliver CEOs or secretaries. Companies couldn't make their production schedules and bankers had less to invest. Markets crashed on the whim of the garbage man who overslept.

Here in the midst of the bustle and the remembered bustle, encumbered by the closeness of strangers, he wondered if part of his rejection of this way of life arose even before he'd met Adriana. The city was supposed to have been their doorway to the world. He'd never meant to settle here.

There was more to it than that, though. He'd grown up in

the Connecticut suburbs with the sarcastic bitterness of his own father's frustrated attempts to be accepted. The pretense of his working-class parents with their stiff dinner parties and constant mimicry of successful neighbors, born to privilege, had poisoned Rhue early to the worthwhile things about sharing your accomplishments or concerns with a supportive community. To his father the end was the important part; the means only the vehicle that took you there.

One June day the summer between fourth and fifth grade, Rhue had bicycled downtown to Best & Company to find the perfect tie for Father's Day. He couldn't have been much more than ten, but he'd been cutting grass for three neighbors and he was flush. Even stuffed with dollars, the coffee can with his money rattled in the metal basket screwed onto his handlebars.

"Swimming at the club today?" His father had pressed him at breakfast, though they'd had a running argument since school let out about Rhue's refusal to join the country club swim team.

"Maybe."

"Did you put those clean clothes away?" His mother anticipated a renewal of the argument.

His father didn't get the hint. "It would build up your shoulders. Girls like broad shoulders."

Rhue had spooned the Cheerios into his mouth and pointed so no answer would be expected.

"I ran into George Hatton at the train station last night and he said Brian's won four blue ribbons already." Although his father addressed his mother, the remark was intended to illustrate the wonderous thrill of beating Brian Hatton who had two pairs of madras shorts and wore a signet ring with his initials, more of the same argument.

"Mrs. Riley needed me to cut her grass, her bridge group was coming to tea."

"Mrs. Riley doesn't run an international corporation like Mr. Hatton does."

"She pays me twenty dollars for an hour."

"Money isn't everything."

"Then why are you always working late? And telling Mom to turn out the lights to keep the electric bill down?"

Behind his father's chair, his mother was leaning against the counter, with the dish towel suspended in the air. Rhue could see the grin on her face reflected in the window. She brought the towel to her lips and bit down to stifle a laugh.

His father put down his fork with the cube of egg and toast still on it. "I didn't mean it that way. Of course money's important, but connections are even more important. I work as hard as I do to ensure that you've got friends like Brian Hatton. You're every bit as smart as the Hattons. You could go to Harvard together, carpool for breaks. His sister's mighty cute."

"Gross, Dad. She has braces and pimples."

"She'll inherit half of George's fortune."

"You told Mom he spent it already on all the silk ties he has."

His father had picked up the plate with the half-eaten breakfast and handed it to his mother. Without speaking he had removed the keys from the rack by the back door and yanked the knob. Over his shoulder he'd called back, "A silk tie is a pretty nice thing to have. I can't afford a silk tie. Someday, when it's too late, you'll wish you had a silk tie or two. When you dress well, people treat you like you're somebody."

The grind of the car engine droned out the rest of the tirade, but Rhue could have finished it himself, he'd heard it so many times.

Rhue's disappearance had forced Ford into the same defensive position. To protect himself, the boy would've had to adopt his mother's view of the world. Not unlike Rip and Wizard, there had been no parent to encourage him to try something different, to be someone different, to rattle expectations, or to ride the monster waves.

Out of necessity, Rip and Wizard were nonconformists already, cognizant of myriad possibilities, eager to find a path no one else had taken. They had the whole world before them. Did they know the journey was the most important thing? As Rhue clumped along in the dusk, he found himself inventing their futures; families and houses and memories for them, where they were happy but also satisfied with what they were capable of contributing.

It was avoidance, he knew. That imagined life was the life with Adriana and Ford that he'd thrown away.

Out West he'd created a life for himself that had seemed real enough; hard weather and harder people, where language and communication meant less than what you could touch and see. Your own awareness and your own conclusions saved you from the rattlesnake at your heel. It was a world without complications, one man against the weather and the wild animals, easier than real life. But without his health, he could no longer fight the elements. His friends were dead or dying. His leg was busted, and his heart was on strike.

Never before had he admitted the dishonesty in what he'd done. He'd told Adriana he wasn't the fatherly type. He'd told himself the same thing. But distance didn't change the fact that he had a son. Although he'd lost time and opportunity, the tie was still there, a marvel in itself. He wondered if the dull raw pain would ever be assuaged. More important still he wondered if meeting Ford after forty years could possibly make a difference. To Ford. Or to him.

After Rhue lost sight of the boys, he clunked along until he reached the spot in the next block where he'd seen them disappear. Two massive stone lions perched atop a simple sign carved in stone, The New York Public Library. Above him on the highest stair, the boys stood shoulder to shoulder, surveying the world.

"Pops?" Wizard called from the automatic door. "We'll be in the computer lab. Mezzanine reading room."

Rhue waved in acknowledgement. He hoped he'd heard them correctly, but he could always ask inside. They hadn't robbed him or beaten him. Like the boys they were, their excitement at being accomplished beyond the adult, at being needed, endeared them to him. While he doubted—from their demeanor and their conversation—that they shared anything worthwhile with their own fathers, he felt a vague and unfamiliar stirring of pride. Problem-solving skills were valuable. Despite their street experience, they could choose not to turn into thugs. Maybe, like him, they would find enough satisfaction in small things to fend off the demons of self-destruction.

Wall signs for the reading room directed him to the elevator. With a fitting library hush, the doors slid open. Leaning back in the cubicle, he took the weight off his bad leg. The change from his hundred-dollar bill at dinner made an awkward lump in the pocket of his jeans, and he wondered again at the ferocity with which he'd saved his money. At first he had wanted not to be in anyone's debt. Independence suited his flight from Adriana. Once he had accumulated a cushion, enough to keep himself in steaks if the jobs fizzled out or the weather turned ugly, he'd tried to spend some of the excess. Tiara's girls liked magazines and baubles. Vince had dragged him to Vegas a time or two, but the sourness of the other gamblers' failures turned his stomach. It was a sad city.

So, he'd opened the bank account and let it draw interest, an unspoken concession to a future time when he might not be able to work. There were plenty of broken cowboys around, playing cards for bourbon, begging for sympathy with stories of rodeos and impromptu boxing matches behind bars. Enough examples of failure to send him hurtling back to cattle drives and rich ranch owners.

One winter when Ford would have been thirteen, Rhue sent a money order to the old New York address. It never came back. He liked to think it paid for a ten-speed bicycle or sailing lessons, something that would give a teenager the same feeling of freedom that riding horseback gave Rhue.

Still, he was surprised Adriana had taken it. He imagined her opening the envelope in an unthinking way, not expecting after all that time to hear from him. She would consider the money. He could see her, in a weak moment, maybe stuck with unexpected bills, folding and refolding the note with the single phrase, "for Ford," and making a split-second decision to keep it. And later—her old anger enflamed at his audacity—she would tear up the note and wish she hadn't accepted anything from him. Not wanting to renew the imagined hurt, he hadn't sent any more.

The library elevator went beyond mezzanine to the top. It started back down again before he realized he'd forgotten to push the button. Where the doors opened, he caught glimpses of glass-covered cases and old chairs with velvet rope across the arms. Preserved history; he couldn't escape it. Yet, this time it was comforting in a strange sense. Its existence and the perpetuation of its sameness. Years and years before his slice of time humans had confronted the edges of the known world and summoned the courage to go beyond. They'd conquered fears bigger than anything he had faced.

Adriana had brought him here once to an exhibition of maps. It had been a rainy Saturday, and they had wandered fascinated through the high-ceilinged rooms for hours before confessing starvation to each other. Unable to decide on a restaurant, they bought pears and cheese and warm bread from the open-air market and took it back to eat on the living room floor. There in the quiet gloom he had made love to her, their whispers filling the room with so much passion he could hardly breathe.

Until then he'd believed there must be a limit to the love a human can feel, but not that day, not with Adriana. And yet it had been three, maybe four months later, in January that he'd left her. Perhaps even during that perfect lazy afternoon, he'd known there would be an end, that, despite the love, he would find the closeness with which she held him to her too claustrophobic after all.

Rip met him at the elevator door. "Man, I was just coming to find you. You are so slow. We found them. You're not going to believe how easy it was."

The thump of the cast on the marble floor startled the other patrons and heads lifted. Rhue felt as if he were processing in a royal entourage the way they all stared as he limped past the rows of oak tables and neat green reading lamps, each lit despite the sunlight that streamed from the clerestory windows two stories above them. Wizard sat cross-legged on an office chair in front of a glowing screen. After Rip dragged over a third chair, he held the back steady while Rhue lowered himself and the cast.

"There she is," Wizard said, pointing to the computer monitor. "Adriana S. Hogan, 78 years old, one son, Ford Simmons Hogan." Underneath the New York Times masthead the headline read, "OBITUARIES."

Chapter Eight

*F*ord's mother's burial was quick. The urn that held her ashes fit neatly into the steel box already set in the newly dug hole. After explaining the federal health regulations, the funeral personnel retreated to their vehicles. Surprising Ford, Evie read a poem she'd written about traveling and coming home. "O Pioneer," she called it, reciting the lines with energetic enthusiasm. Afterward, after the ceremonial shovelful of dirt covered the top of the urn, she thrust the curled copy in his hand and left him to say his own private good-bye. When it was over and the funeral personnel departed, he was surprised again to find her wandering among the old stones.

"Some of these graves are more than three hundred years old," she said.

"Hmmm." He could see human life like a long string weaving in and out of history, the continuity of families, endless spooling generations of grandfathers and fathers and sons.

"I found a bunch of Simmonses."

"Mom will be comfortable then."

"Depends how much she liked her relatives."

He could feel Evie watching him for signs of emotional breakdown.

"I'm not going to cry, if you're worried. Real men don't cry."

"The hell they don't."

"Look, you've been great. The poem was great. Touching. I appreciate your effort at helping me grieve. But old people die. It was the right thing to happen. I'm fine with her dying."

"Okay, already." Her voice was tinny and barely audible, the music gone. She wrapped her arms around her middle and stared at the headstones spread out across the hillside. "I'll wait at the car."

After she tromped off, he kicked the loose gravel with the heel of his hiking boot. He walked the opposite direction from the car. Looking back from the next block of graves, his scuffmarks were visible in the lane. His boots, soaked from the dewy grass, collected mud in heavy clumps. In an irregular pattern he moved through the graveyard, careful to wipe his muddy soles on the grass in between the graves. His inner compass kept his mother's grave in the center of his perambulations.

Evie confounded him. His mother, too, would have been confused. As he should have expected, he moved through life as his mother had moved, changing direction and backtracking when the path became too difficult. Not at all like Evie who walked in straight lines, discovering the patterns as she experienced them as if they were created solely to give her pleasure. To Evie, life was simple.

By the time he reached the car, he was sorry to the point of despair. The poem had been more than lovely, spare and elegant like his mother on her best days. It amazed him Evie could have discerned that from the little he had spoken of his mother.

"So now you know what a jerk I am," he said to her back where she leaned against the far side of the car.

"I knew before."

It took him a minute to recover. She was making it hard to apologize.

"I can't ask you to forgive me. What I did was unforgivable." He stopped, hoping she would contradict him, fix what he'd ruined. When she didn't, he forced himself to speak. "Do you want to go home?"

"Home?" When she turned, he could see she'd been crying, but more than that, he saw a soft vulnerability in her cheeks and eyelids, something she was struggling to handle, but that she assumed he couldn't understand. She wasn't quite frowning, more perplexed. "New York may be home for you, but . . ."

His fingers ached to spot the tears that fell down her cheeks and onto the uneven ground of the newly mowed graves, but he'd lost that right. Or maybe never earned it.

Taking careful note of the signs so he didn't get them lost, he drove back to the Cove Inn without speaking. The sun, creeping out from the lingering ocean mist, coated the air with a dusty filtered light like the gauze sheath of a Middle Eastern dancer, mysterious and enticing. As he parked the car, he stole a quick look at Evie. She sat trance-like, her hands in her lap.

"Evie?"

She didn't answer.

"I'm sorry for what happened out there."

She had to hear the confusion and sorrow in his voice, but she just reached out and, without expression or reply, opened the car door. In the same amnesiac stupor she walked to their room. Ten paces behind her he hurried to unlock the door. Inside she removed her sweater and disappeared into the bathroom. The toilet flushed. The shower ran.

After taking off his shoes and putting them on a piece of newspaper to dry, he sat on the extra bed and waited. He didn't want to trivialize what had happened by turning on the television or sleeping. Women were inexplicable. Not that he didn't know how brusque he'd sounded. He knew she was sensitive to criticism despite her sense of humor. He'd meant to show her he was being mature about losing his mother. That was all.

But was it? He searched his life for clues that might lead him to a clearer understanding of the sabotage he caused for himself. His mind skipped from recent events to long distant memories and back again. Leaden clouds clung to the line of smooth ocean as if they were attached below the surface and any rend might allow the world to slide through and disappear. He tried to think back to a truly happy moment in his childhood, a point in time without any confusion, without any hovering shadows or doubts.

He remembered being thirteen and being thrilled when his mother gave him permission to ride the subway by himself. More than his brain, his body remembered the easy lope down two flights of stairs, the eager hiss of the mechanical doors, the rush of legs and feet and arms into the havoc of riders departing and entering, the sharp light above his head as he climbed the stairs and stood on a strange new stretch of sidewalk in a place he'd never before walked.

But there was also the image of his mother's creased forehead at the living room window where he'd imagined she waited, worrying over his safety. She'd glance up from a magazine she was pretending to read, forever convinced he'd been kidnapped, never to return.

He pushed back farther in his mind. There was a day when several fathers took a bunch of the neighborhood boys to a ball game. His mother gave him money for a T-shirt, and that reassurance weighted down his pocket. He felt grown-up, the only one without a parent supervising him. The sharp smell of mustard heated in the sun, and the edgy crowd, elbows and hips bumping his shoulders when they stood and screamed at the tiny white ball soaring over a sea of green and into a void of hats and waving arms; that had been a perfect day.

Until he'd overheard two of the men talking about his mother, how pretty she was and how ripe for the picking, without a man for all those years. He'd been sullen and quiet the rest of the trip, mad at his mother for being attractive and mad at his father for everything else that was wrong with the world, including the home team's loss that day.

His earlier memories were jumbled and harder to hold on to; the apartment before the house on Long Island, his first day of kindergarten when his mother cried in front of everyone in the class, and the holiday visits of her parents who stopped coming when he was seven without explanation. It wasn't until he was graduated from college that he understood his mother had grown tired of listening to their suggestions about available men. She'd never conceded marriage as the only way of life, that much he'd understood from her anger at Rhue.

Once when he was on college break, he asked her about the point when dating turned into something more serious.

"You're nowhere close to that," she said, keeping her hands busy with the salad preparations, and at his hurt look, "You'll know when it happens."

"But the girls I date want to dictate where we go. They don't like my suggestions."

"Someday there'll be one who will."

"So I just go on making the suggestions and arguing with them."

"If you're arguing, you ought to try someone else."

"I don't want a girl who has no opinions."

"In the right relationship there's a balance." She stopped chopping scallions and analyzed his face. He felt as if she were realizing for the first time that he might make a mistake and there was nothing she could do about it. But she'd surprised him by saying, "You have to trust your instincts."

He'd gone out that night and been tongue-tied at the young poli sci major who was convinced that within two decades the world would be unified under the Chinese government. She'd offered to go to bed with him if he attended the nuclear disarmament rally with her the next night, but he had a chem test the morning after and so they parted without animosity.

Although he liked that about her, he wasn't sure continued compromise on issues that big would have left them much time together.

When he wasn't being prickly about Evie's amazing ability to read his emotional barometer, he realized he had more shared interests with her than any of the women he'd dated. None of his former girlfriends or his male friends had the same knack at understanding him. Evie's insight kept him off balance, which was not necessarily bad. When the motel shower stopped running, the silence stunned him. He checked his watch. Only twenty minutes, but, with his whole life revisited, he felt as if years had passed. He rubbed his eyes. He swung his arms to wake up. He had no idea how to explain to her what he was afraid of, mostly because he wasn't sure himself.

Maybe he could convince her to swim again. They had missed lunch. If he could find a harborside restaurant, the boats might distract her. He could start again and try to recapture the sense of adventure that had drawn them together.

"Ford?" She whispered when she emerged, dressed, but barefoot. "I need to talk to you."

She sat next to him on the bed, close enough that their legs touched. Her hair curled in deep wet swirls. He could smell soap and vanilla. Afraid that whatever he said would be wrong, he didn't speak. The urge to put his arms around her and draw her close built inside until he could hardly stand it. Their shoulders touched, and after several more silent minutes, she slumped against him, her chin lowered to her chest. Praying silently in short spurts of repetitive phrases, he asked God to inspire him to say the right thing, to show him what to do.

When she began to talk, her words were filled with something indescribable and pure. Like honey flowing from an overturned jar, the words poured clear and thick with meaning and truth. She talked about being a little girl and thinking of all the hard, brave things grownups did that she would never be able to do, and then how her mother had told her she could do them if she wanted to badly enough, how love would make it easier.

"This is what my mother meant, I think."

Ford's arm, with its own momentum, went around her shoulders so that the two of them formed a cocoon of words and limbs. "This?" he asked, thinking he knew what she meant at the same time that he wished he knew for sure.

"I love you."

"I love you, too."

Tighter and tighter they held onto each other until they were spinning in each other's arms, in the story of her past and his childhood and their future, so fast that their clothes fell away with the centrifugal force of their feelings and they were making love in a tight circle inside each other, whirling and turning and spinning in a tiny world of their own filled with songs and warm breezes and the most delicious sweetness.

The phone was ringing. Twenty, thirty times it rang before he untangled from her arms and answered it. The sunshine had faded, its spidery fingertips just letting go of the curtains to make way for the evening. By the time he replaced the receiver, Evie was awake. She traced her fingers along his shoulders and back in a slow drawl of longing that made him ache with wonder.

When he kissed her, she moaned in reply, the vibrations, far away and inside him at the same time. If he closed his eyes, they could be frozen like this forever, no past, no future, only present perfection, lovers in perpetuity.

But when he stopped for a breath, she squirmed free and repositioned the pillow to look at him. "So. Who was it?"

"Maurice," he said, wishing he'd let it ring.

She looked back quizzically. "Maurice found us here?"

"He called the funeral home."

"What's the matter?"

"He says I need to come back to New York." As curious as she'd been from the beginning, he thought she would argue, complain, demand reasons, but she didn't. She smiled instead and tickled his neck with her lips.

He stood and strode across the room. He flung open the single window and drank in the world, the glistening pool, the sterling dusk with its rusted furrows of good weather predicted, the small spots of painted color in the garden. He felt huge, powerful, like a god able to gather in all that he saw and hold it in his hand next to his furiously beating heart. He didn't want to go back. He didn't want to go anywhere.

"He's probably overreacting," Evie said.

"Don't you want to know what it's all about?"

She shook her head. "I'm a gypsy, remember?"

"I didn't say I was going."

"Oh, well, I'm okay with that too. Maurice is a big boy. He can figure out how to handle whatever it is."

"Not this. It's my father." When her face started to crumple in pain lines, pain for him, pain from pain, he cupped her chin in his hands. "It's not what you think. He's in New York."

"He's not dead?"

He shook his head. The words bounced in the little room like a squash ball out of control.

"Is he okay?"

"What difference does that make?" His anger surprised him. He'd thought, during the discovery of the photos and his mother's vagueness and refusal to help him understand, that his father's absence was simply a geographical fact. While his father was his father, they didn't know each other and therefore any possible correlation was negated.

But now the one fact had been replaced with the fact of his existence within Ford's piece of space and time. Ford saw that a father, even an absent father, might be a psychological factor in your development as a person. He'd lost the one person who might have given him some insight on how to handle Rhue's appearance. Or reappearance. With only himself to rely on, being angry was getting in the way.

Evie seemed not to notice. "He's not just a man who deserted his family. He's a man too. You don't know what happened back then. You said yourself your mother refused to talk about it. Maybe there were extenuating circumstances. Don't you care?"

"Care? I don't even know him."

"Here's your chance. He's called you, he must want to know you."

"A little late."

"How can you not see him after all this time when he's making such an effort?"

"He made his choice."

"Maybe he didn't know your mom was expecting."

"He knew. She said he knew." He slugged the pillow and fell on the bed, almost crushing her. He wanted to burrow back in the cocoon of their lovemaking and forget the world beyond the green and gold room in New England. He should have known something would happen to ruin things. He should have known his father would be at the root of it.

Humming to herself, Evie kneaded his shoulders. She nuzzled his ear and kissed his eyebrows and the bones in his spine. He thought he might cry. He was ashamed that he was so selfish, but he knew that's what it was. His life was his own finally, more so with his mother gone. Here he was, presenting it to Evie who seemed perfectly satisfied with his muddled self, even though he was still trying to decipher what about him she found interesting. The complications of merging two independent lives would be difficult enough without a newfound father in their midst.

All this time Rhue had stayed away. Why couldn't he have waited a little longer so Ford would have time to work Evie into his life? He wanted it so badly and he didn't do it well. And now she would wonder—looking at his twenty years alone, the string of half-done relationships—was he like his father? Did he mean what he said? Would he too leave her someday?

He tried to recreate the resolve he'd felt after his mother died. Buried in the sheets with Evie, he lay still and let the heat from her limbs flow into his. He could feel himself floating, treading water, with the swirling ocean all around him. The little boat blended into the horizon and disappeared.

Chapter Nine

Outside the library Rhue put his hand on the wall that lipped the steps and worked himself, step by step, down to street level. The leg was so stiff he had to steel himself before lowering it. The pain shot into his hip each time he put the least weight on it. When he paused, he found himself listening for his heart, worried that the strain of keeping up with the boys, moving too fast, would bring on another stroke, or worse. He'd never worried before about his health. It had been a given like the weather and the mountains on the horizon. Even in the hospital he hadn't worried about his body, only that he'd lost days without anything to show for it. But the slap of Adriana's death had softened him.

Ahead of him he heard the boys' voices, less sure too, disappointed at their failure to deliver what they'd promised. His own disappointment seemed less significant compared to theirs, and he marveled again at their instant loyalty to a stranger. It was a measure of what they'd never had within their own families, he guessed.

"Friggin' dead," Rip muttered to Wizard. "What a waste. What's he going to do now?"

"The super said, the son's gone north? What the hell is that supposed to mean?"

"It doesn't make any difference. It's too messy. At least if his old lady loved him once, she might have helped the kid understand, but without her . . . the old man won't last the night. Waiting for the guy, wondering if he's coming or not, he'll change his mind." Rip bolted down the steps two at a time. "The cowboy's going to fold."

Once he reached them, Rhue sucked in enough air to reply without conveying his own disappointment. "You guys go ahead. I'll find a hotel. Tomorrow I can make some calls."

Neither boy answered. Rip, having reached the sidewalk, stood like a boulder braced against the stream of fleeing businessmen armed with briefcases. It was rush hour. Strangers charged forward, heads down, dogged in their determination to best the people at their heels and beat them to the corner. In the flow of shoulders and legs, Rip's body made a small island that forced the foot traffic around them. He turned and spoke to Wizard on the bottom step.

"Anyway we've got school in the morning."

"Hang school," Wizard hissed at Rip. "We can't leave him. The rodents'll eat him alive."

When they took Rhue's elbows again, he didn't ask questions. He just let them lead him away from the library as if he had no willpower of his own. He didn't watch which direction they were going. Adriana dead? It was impossible. He would have felt something. According to the obituary she'd been dead only four days. He'd been leaving the hospital, or maybe just boarding the train when she'd died. Why hadn't he known? Sensed that she was no longer in this world? The cast bumped on the cement as they moved with the throngs along the sidewalk. He winced with every step.

Tiara and her girls and every woman he'd ever made love to, they'd been stand-ins for Adriana. He saw it now. Each time he'd said hello, he'd been comparing them to her. That's why he never stayed with any of them. He'd rarely gone back to the same one. No one had ever matched up. He'd even held Marian at arms' length, though she'd never been his lover, only a soul mate. She, at least, had understood the need for distancing, the value in doing a job well and moving on. She'd loved the horses in the same way, for their ability to maintain their independence.

He didn't turn around to read the street signs, afraid that if he did, the tiredness that leaked from him as he limped along in this makeshift human sling, might have left a trail on the sidewalk like blood. If the Clark kid and the other ranch hands could see him, they'd think he was broke, as bad off as a branded steer. And if Rip and Wizard took his money, so be it. He didn't belong here, never had.

Trying to change something once it was done was a pipe dream. With the horses, he'd always known that, but Vince's death had confused him, made him think that a person could redirect the consequences of his own actions if he wanted something badly enough. He'd been fooling himself with Delilah. Maybe it wasn't the first time.

A vision appeared in his mind of Marian the second or third winter they'd driven cattle south and considered spending the dead months in Mexico together. Vince had left that morning; a sister's wedding or new baby, Rhue couldn't remember. Marian's back was to him. They were both repacking saddlebags, joking about Vince's agitation over what to wear for a formal occasion, when her voice had gone all quiet and low, then stopped altogether. He'd turned to see why and found her staring at him.

"What?" he'd said, noting the bronze of her cheeks against the white serape and the grace of her long legs above the boots.

"Do you ever think about …" her lips tightened and her hands poised above the horse, a silent movie pose of indecision. This happened so rarely that he interrupted her. So great was his fear that she was going to say something about the two of them and he wouldn't know how to respond, he cut her off.

"The girth's a little loose," he said, the kind of random remark he would have expected from one of the younger hands, a show-off type of statement to establish who was the expert here. A chicken's way of changing the subject. Without another word, she swung herself into the saddle and dug her heels into the horse's belly. When he called to her to wait, she didn't reply. He told himself she hadn't heard him, but he knew it wasn't true. The look in her eyes haunted him enough that he drank too much at Tiara's and danced until the fiddler quit and everyone else disappeared upstairs. With the snow just starting to drift into the corners of the windowsills, he convinced one of the new girls to ride with him to Tijuana where she stayed until her laugh frayed his nerves and he sent her home on the train. Perhaps

Marian in the deepest recesses of her dementia was still wondering if they would have made good dance partners.

Four, eight, ten blocks later—it seemed like hours to Rhue—the boys settled him in the shadows of an abandoned warehouse. He balanced on a pile of dismantled cardboard boxes, damp from rain, and soggy to the touch. The boys huddled together just out of his hearing, black hulking shadows against the empty parking lot. They worked in the dark at a side door and eventually he heard the lock spring; the snap of metal, a dead giveaway. After checking over their shoulders, they edged back to him, pulled him inside, and jammed an iron bar against the doorknob.

"Your basic New York security system," Rip offered, laughing at his own joke, though Rhue was awake again, busy examining the space. They had him alone, where no one could see him. If he disappeared, no one would find him for months, maybe years.

Through the unlit first floor the boys skirted piles of debris and salted circles left over from stagnant puddles. They led him to an old freight elevator. With a jerry-rigged pulley and the two of them straining, they managed, choking and gagging, to lift him onto the partial platform of what had once been an elevator car. Then they raised the car itself through the shaft to the second floor. He didn't ask where they were and they didn't say.

After they maneuvered him to an old couch, they huddled again to whisper as if he might be asleep and they didn't want to wake him. The couch had a stale odor, hard to place, but not particularly unpleasant. None of the cushions matched. Three cupboards, with pieces of ripped sheetrock still hanging from the edges, stood like islands in the room. Their conference ended, they stared at the wall for several minutes without looking at him. Rhue wondered if they were summoning courage for some violence against him.

His heart, though, remained steady, almost too slow. The adrenaline of anxiety didn't come, which surprised him. He wondered if he was so subconsciously wedded to Adriana that her death obviated his will to live. Perhaps that explained his waltzing through all those years with the horses, avoiding a permanent connection to any of the women he'd tried like pies in a county fair contest, praising them, but never taking one home. It might be easier on all of them if he just died. They could leave him here for the warehouse rats.

A tidy combination of Marian and Vince at the last, sinking into death, no struggle, no guilt, no mourners, and no memories. Ford, wherever he was, however he lived, would continue on his own way as he must already have done. Competent Adriana would have brooked no dependent son, despite her husband's flight from responsibility or maybe because of it. Depression sat him like a cowhand sat his horse at the end of the trail. Trapped and fenced after miles of open plain, the cattle lowed good-byes to a life they knew instinctively was over. And the idea of real beds and perfumed hands floated in the dusty swirls of the cowboys' exhaustion.

When Rhue looked up, Rip's hand was inside one of the cupboards, his side blocking Rhue's view. The perfect hiding place for a weapon. Rhue expected the worst and struggled to clear his head to defend himself. But still his old man's heart dribbed and drabbed as if it hardly needed the blood to continue pumping. If this was the end, he would let it happen. What was the point with Adriana gone?

Rip produced a coffeepot from the shelf, and even then Rhue hardly paid attention. In practiced motions, the boy plugged it into a wall socket over by the single window and poured water from an old milk carton into it. Ignoring Rhue, the boys continued to pull things from cupboards and random cardboard boxes with apparent purpose. A blanket went up over the single metal casement window, rippling a wide red swathe on the grubby block wall. Their energy made him tired. He closed his eyes and tried to imagine an afterlife with canyons.

The coffeemaker was buzzing when he woke up. The boys were sitting on the floor, side by side, opposite the couch. Rip nudged Wizard when Rhue straightened up.

Crackers and peanut butter had appeared on top of one of the cupboards with a plastic knife and a paper plate. Wizard scooted the whole cupboard closer to their guest.

"Appetizers," he offered, grinning. "We stay here some when we need a safe house." One palm turned upward in supplication to indicate the seriousness of the revelation. "No one knows."

"Safe from what?" Rhue asked, flexing his shoulder as he came out of his stupor now that he'd had a nap.

In delayed acknowledgement of the question, Rip laughed. "Man, you shouldn't ask stuff like that. We got reputations, you know. We can't tell you everything."

Rhue considered asking about their mothers. Wouldn't they

worry if the boys didn't come home for dinner? But as soon as he thought it, he understood how ridiculous it would sound. Streetwise, Rip and Wizard lived in a different world. In spite of the slip about Wizard's father, they'd been careful to keep the two worlds separate. Even they recognized Rhue didn't belong here.

"Are you a cowboy for real?" Wizard asked once they'd eaten half the peanut butter.

"Yeah."

"You ride horses and all?"

"Yeah."

"Ever run into a coyote?"

So he told them stories about the cattle drives to Texas and the mountain lions and Tiara's Titty Palace. Marian fascinated them and they asked for more stories about the Indians.

After an hour Rip apologized for interrupting. "We gotta go. You're fine here for the night. I'm sorry about dinner. Too risky to cook with the electricity, it's a little, ah, irregular."

Wizard set a glass jar by the couch. "Portable john."

"You rest. We'll bring you a big breakfast."

"Hey, sir?" Wizard called up the elevator shaft, "You don't need medicine for that leg, do you?"

"No, and don't steal any."

Both boys laughed. Rhue closed his eyes, not sure what had earned him the "sir." The grinding of the elevator cables under the weight of the cage and the echoing footsteps carried up the shaft to him, hollow and empty sounds in the filtered warehouse night. He realized, with the elevator pulley set on the first floor position, he was imprisoned until the boys returned, but he was so tired he didn't care. It was very possible he was safer here than wherever the boys were going.

Unbidden, his mind traveled back to that last evening with Delilah. In his exhaustion it was the last thing he remembered with utter clarity, the lightheaded anticipation of the ride, the heat of her shoulders under his thighs. He drifted, in and out of sleep, skyscrapers and suspension bridges superimposed on rolling hills and striated cliffs, all noiseless except for the hazy remembered whistle of wind in tall grass and drumming hooves on dry earth.

He had to drag his mind back to the present. Tomorrow would be his second day in the city, a second chance to finish what he'd come for. Through the charity listed in the obituary, soliciting donations in lieu of flowers, the boys had finagled the name of Ford's employer. Dialing for Rhue, they'd handed off the library pay phone to him. He'd been forwarded to the personnel department. The girl there, with some cajoling, had given him the number of Ford's apartment building. After the superintendent's initial suspicion, he'd been cooperative. Without promising anything, the fellow said he might be able to get word to Ford wherever it was he'd gone up north. Although it wasn't an ideal way to inform a son that his phantom father existed, it was done.

Rhue was too tired to worry about any of it. If Ford came back, they would meet. If he didn't, Rhue would buy a train ticket to some place new. He'd done it before. He could do it again.

In the middle of the night, he awakened to a skittering close at hand. He surveyed the floor, but nothing moved. Moonlight illuminated the room, rendering the nondescript walls and floor a soft rose-tinged peat that reminded him of the canyon corridors they'd raced chasing wild ponies. He blinked. More scratching sounds came from the first floor below his feet. Using the closest cabinet for leverage, he pulled himself to standing and moved haltingly across the moonbeams to the window. Pulling back a corner of the red cloth, he looked out on a wide lawn of empty parking lot to a street without cars.

The crackling grew louder. A raccoon? Rats? He turned back to the appetizer cupboard, unable to remember whether Rip had closed the peanut butter jar. In a place like this any hint of food would draw animals.

A sharp movement in the elevator shaft startled him. When it repeated, it reflected on the steel walls of the elevator. He smelled something. Flames. The air popped and hissed. Something on the first floor was burning. The fire, crackling with energy and a craving for oxygen, was spreading.

Even if the elevator car were on this level, even if he could work the pulley by himself, smoke was already seeping up through the open shaft. Heated beyond endurance, greedy fingers of flame poked and stretched along the cables toward the second floor hideaway. It was impossible to leave the way he'd come. He moved back, shuffling and slow at first until his muscles warmed. Like a blind person, his hands extended on the walls, he traced the outline of the room, looking for a door, hoping for stairs. He kept his eye on the wall with the elevator gate. Slivers of fire sparked and filled the cracks in the metal casing to remind him the fire was getting closer.

Smoke insinuated itself into his nostrils and mouth. Coughing, he choked on smoke and air and smoke again. Despite his groping, the walls were smooth. Other than the elevator, no exits, secret or otherwise. When he reached the far side of the window, he had to admit he was trapped. Although the flames seemed to be isolated just below the floor and outside the elevator shaft, they lit the square opening in the wall with their intensity. His shirt, soaked with perspiration, clung to his chest and arms like a second skin. In what he hoped was a calm voice, he shouted for help, reciting his location above the freight elevator over and over.

Sirens came out of the blue from the north, almost as if they had been switched on only within sight of the flames. He ripped down the curtain and stared. Through the grimy panes of the single window he counted six or seven engines as they circled into position. Heaving the peanut butter jar, he tried to break the glass, but the jar bounced back into the room, barely skimming his head. Metal filaments laced the thick pane, industrial strengtheners to keep out the bad guys.

His feet felt warm—he hoped it was his imagination—and he could see where the heat was warping the scrolls of ironwork on the elevator gate even though the flames had not yet reached the second floor. As he stared at the amassing crowd of fire fighters on the pavement below, he considered the building opposite him. As close as it was, the two warehouses didn't appear to be connected. No escape route that way.

Even before the firemen's ladders were extended, the hoses, like machine-gun fire, sprayed against the far side of the building. At that distance no one would hear him. And no one would see him through the second story window. His mind raced through the possibilities. If Rip and Wizard had chosen this safe house for its proximity to their real homes, they might see or hear the commotion and get word to someone about him. It was his only hope.

As the smoke rose and infiltrated the room, he began to feel dizzy. Bending to the window ledge, his lips opened to the small crack and the fresh air.

He should have died on the prairie that night, the wind at his back, he and Delilah locked in their last dance. If he were a praying man, he would ask God about the irony of letting him survive the stroke and come East only to die alone in a forgotten warehouse, hours away from seeing his only son for the first time. Adriana and he had debated many times the existence of a God. She'd conceded to his atheism each time, perhaps sensing his need to avoid dependence on something outside himself, but he wasn't at all sure he had convinced her or himself.

He'd been adamant that each man made his own way. It had given him comfort during his campfire musings, so far away from the son growing up without a father. To himself, when he was too wired to sleep, which didn't happen often, he would calculate the myriad ways a boy would be stronger for having no father dictate his manners, his education, his lifestyle. It raised the specter of his own father more often than Rhue might otherwise have summoned those memories.

Gerald Hogan had been weighed down with the fear of failure. His son Rhue had not realized it until the time for empathy was long past. Saturday after Saturday Rhue's father had donned the country club costume and gone to play golf. Although he hated the game and couldn't afford the expense, he envied the other businessmen their easy camaraderie, their slender blonde wives, their tennis-playing children. Saturday nights, despite a long series of complaints about sore muscles, wasted greens fees, or another player's crude jokes or graphic tales of secret liaisons at the office, Gerald Hogan would insist his wife and son dress in their Sunday best and accompany him to dinner at the club.

"Cheryl, you're not listening to me." The arguments would filter down the hallway of their oh-so-smart suburban split level to their son's bedroom. "These men are community leaders. They're running Fortune 500 companies. Success breeds success."

"They don't care about you."

"That's irrelevant. If they see us there, they'll think of me when they need insurance. For God's sake, Cheryl, we're so close. If you would only make friends with their wives, sign Rhue up for tennis lessons, we'd be there."

Nine-year-old Rhue, thirteen-year-old Rhue, sixteen-year-old Rhue would listen to his father's voice weep frustration, even in all its belligerence, and wonder why his father didn't see the way those same men talked about him behind his back, about his Filene's basement ties, his second-hand car, his hand-drawn advertisements in the club bulletin.

Rhue's refusal to play tennis or wear madras shorts or date the right daughter had been made apologetically, without aggressiveness, without explanation, because he was afraid his father would have died if he'd known the truth. But when his father continued to scrape and bow, Rhue's decision to choose a different life for himself became easier. He wanted to change the system, to make the world a place where people could be celebrated for individual personalities and talents, a place where Gerald Hogan would have been welcomed as a good provider with a willing and enthusiastic heart. It was a dream Rhue had pursued so vigorously that he'd lost perspective as badly as his father had.

A sharp crack brought Rhue back to the present. Whether it was the heat or the flames moving up the first floor walls, the window glass split in several diagonal lines and outside air rushed in. Methodically, but as fast as he dared, he pushed out the slivers with a sofa cushion and created a space large enough to squeeze through. But when his skin bumped the metal, the sting sizzled. He hobbled back to the coffeepot, felt along the floor until he found the water jug, and brought it back to the window. The dribbled water spit and sang on the warm metal. He'd have to move quickly. After wrestling his head and shoulders, he scanned the outside of the warehouse, looking for inspiration. Running just beside the window were the metal rungs of a ladder built onto the wall like water tower steps. He'd been so busy looking for a way down, the way he'd come, he hadn't thought about going up.

With his hands wrapped in fabric he'd ripped from the couch, he gripped the top of the window frame and eased his body out, avoiding the metal frame as best he could. He stretched his arms, grabbed the closest rung and wiggled until his lower body fell loose. The fabric of his jeans ripped, leaving one lone blue scrap on the window frame. He let his legs fall against the wall, finding a toehold for the good leg on the rung just below the window. Sharp intake of breath at the reverberating pain in his bad ankle, quicker swallow of the sweeping dizziness that rose up at the open air between him and the ground.

While he couldn't see any flames on this side of the building, he could hear it snarling and hissing. With no clear view in the smoke of whether the steps reached the ground level, he couldn't risk starting down, only to be caught in escaping flames. Up was his only choice.

The tanker trucks pumped furiously, their rhythmic bangs filled the gray void below him. Once the firemen with the hoses rounded the corner someone would spot him climbing to the roof. He wasn't sure whether to be relieved at the prospect or not. A stranger with no local ties would be considered a prime suspect in a warehouse fire.

The cast created a more immediate problem. It was too thick to allow him to fit his toes on the narrow rungs and then step up with the other foot. Each time he moved upward with his hands, he had to let the bad leg hang and jump the good leg onto the next bar. His knee slammed into the rungs in between and he cried out with every move, though the roaring fire muffled the noises he made, rendering them insignificant as soon as they were uttered.

Once, on a dare with Vince, he'd climbed a water tower one hand tied behind his back. He'd had to let go of each rung and grab the next in that split second of separation. Vince had come behind him with the same handicap, ribbing him all the way. They'd paraded around the top of the tank like roosters, proud not only of being able to do it, but of being tough enough to try. When the sheriff came with his bullhorn and ordered them down, they'd felt foolish though, as if they were teenagers on the loose.

The edge of the warehouse roof was still two stories above him.

"Hey, Cowboy," Rip's head popped out of a third floor window some distance above him. "Up here, hurry."

After eight more crashing steps, Rhue's armpits were close enough for Rip to reach out and drag him inside.

"Didn't you hear us banging on the floor?" Without stopping for an answer Rip motioned for Rhue to follow.

At the far end of the room, four times as long as the second floor "safe" room, Wizard beckoned from outside an open door, his silhouette defined by the arched lights of a distant bridge. Behind Wizard the metal steps of a rusted fire escape glistened. The boys must have come up that way.

They climbed down, swinging Rhue between them to save time and to keep the weight off his leg. At the bottom they paused behind a rusted front end loader to plot a route that would avoid the manic circling of the emergency lights. The voice behind the bullhorn would have questions, impossible questions for a traveling man from Montana and for two hoodlum boys without fathers to stand by them.

Chapter Ten

When Ford opened his eyes, Evie was awake, staring into his. He wound a loose lock of her hair around his finger.

"Glad you came?" he whispered close to her ear.

"Sounds like you're fishing for a compliment."

He kissed her on her lips, her nose, her eyelids, her lips again. "I don't know where you came from or why, but I can't imagine going anywhere ever again without you."

"Wow. That's the most you've ever said in one sitting."

"You inspire me."

She wrinkled her nose. "I can't believe I've fallen for a geek who speaks Hallmark."

He tickled her until she screamed for him to stop. "Okay, wench, get up. No more nice guy. We've left most of New England out of our tour and it needs seeing."

"What about your dad? You just gonna leave him waiting in New York?"

He'd been trying to forget, trying to gather in all the wonder of Evie, but he knew that she was right. He had to make a decision.

"Today we're doing shipyards and seamen's museums. We can talk about my father tonight."

When it seemed to satisfy her, he was relieved.

"Ten minutes," she announced as she shut the bathroom door. When he tried to make love to her in the shower, she pushed him out and barred the door with her hip. "Go away. When I'm hungry, I get mean."

As he pulled on khakis and an old button down shirt, he wondered again about his father's motivation at this late date. A reasonable person would have telephoned in advance, or written a letter. At the least a reasonable person would have apologized before appearing at someone's doorstep. Maybe Evie was right, maybe his father was dying, sick with an uncurable illness, his time running out.

Mad all over again at being forced into a course of action he might not have chosen if he'd had time to consider, he told himself he had every right to take his own time to decide. Reasonable people didn't make split second decisions. But even so, the truth was he would have to make this decision eventually and he was simply buying time with Evie to avoid making it. He was as selfish as his father had been forty years ago.

Wrapped in two of the motel's skimpy towels she emerged minutes later, her face flushed pink like the palest rose. He fell in love all over again. What he wanted more than anything was to proclaim his feelings to a crowded room as if saying them in public would cement the relationship so that not even he could ruin it. She dressed in front of him with an abandon he envied, but years of living alone had cost him that kind of natural spontaneity. Feeling awkward and out of sync and hoping she hadn't noticed, he went outside and then called through the closed door, "I'm going over to the front desk to get a map."

Downtown Marblehead was deserted until they reached Front Street, which ran the length of the harbor. Chugging fishing boats maneuvered into spaces at the floating wooden docks. In rough voices men in rubber pants pronounced numbers as they heaved great buckets of squirming silver into the holding tanks on the docks. An odd collection of women, some in hair rollers and others in pastel leather shoes, lined up on the stone landing to haggle with the fishermen.

Arm in arm, Ford and Evie watched the whiskered men joke among themselves as they grabbed fish and chopped off heads and tails in smooth effortless motions. Using their aproned bellies as an extra pair of hands, they wrapped the trimmed fish in newspaper, creating neat packages in seconds. They presented the wrapped fish to the ladies as if they were offering diamonds. Several boys ran back and forth from the dock to the landing, carting fish and crabs in smaller plastic tubs.

When one boy slipped and slid, feet first, down the ramp on his stomach, the fishermen laughed. Evie ran and knelt by him, shouldering him by the arm until he regained his balance. For the briefest minute their heads bent together, and then she ruffled his hair and returned to Ford.

"He's ten. He works here every morning, then goes to school. The teacher excuses his tardiness because his father drowned last winter."

"He volunteered all that? He doesn't look like the type who'd beg for sympathy."

"I asked him."

Moving past the crowded wharf, she left Ford standing alone. What was she trying to tell him? Something important he felt. Important for them, for their future. Perplexed, he stayed where she'd left him and analyzed the boy. Compact and muscular, he moved more slowly than the others, his feet placed cautiously on the slippery decking. When the other boys raced by, he looked up, shaking his head as if he hated to let them beat him, but he didn't change his pace because of it. At the top of the ramp the tub he was carrying tilted for a second. Ford, close enough, grabbed the edge and righted it. A long drip of seawater splashed over his shoes.

The boy shifted the container on his thigh. "Sorry."

"Glad to help." Ford pretended to examine the fish. "How much do you get for doing this?"

"They pay by the load." The boy gestured with his head to the fishermen in the boats.

"How many loads in one morning?"

"Depends."

"Try me."

"Thirty on a good day. I have algebra at ten o'clock, so I have to leave then no matter how busy they are. They don't like that."

"Screw 'em. Algebra's important. Someday you'll be lending them money for new boats and then they'll understand the value of algebra." Ford continued to follow the boy as he delivered the load, stepped over the pile of wide-eyed heads, grabbed an empty tub by the top of the ramp, and started down for another batch.

"How much for each load?" he asked as the boy passed him.

"Fifty cents."

"Fifteen bucks a day . . ."

"A hundred and five a week."

"They fish on Sundays?"

"Except hurricane season."

"And the money? It's for your mother?"

"Your girlfriend tell you that?"

"Yeah. But I guess you keep a little for yourself. Saving for something special?" The boy looked so guilty that Ford regretted asking. "I used to do that too, out of the grocery money. My father didn't die, though, he just walked out."

Ford dug his hands into the slippery carcasses and dumped them into the tub, copying the boy who moved twice as fast. He tried to remember when he was the age of this kid, whether having to fend for himself had made him resent his father more. But his memories centered on his mother and his friends, as if a father were simply a thing you had or not, like a certain kind of bicycle. He didn't remember feeling lost back then without a father to teach him things.

When the tub was full, Ford took one side of the tub and they walked it up the ramp, unintentionally blocking the way for returning boys.

"Marco, you, turd." A boy with a crew cut hissed from the top.

Ford positioned himself between the toughie and Marco. "Watch your mouth."

"Yeah, who says?"

Ford made a fist inside his coat pocket, finger extended toward the toughie, and raised the corner of his jacket like a gun. "His uncle Tommy from Chicago, that's who. Who wants to argue with Uncle Tommy?"

"No one I know," the kid mumbled and waited until they were clear before he trooped down the ramp. He didn't look back.

"Listen," Ford spoke under his breath at the side of Marco's head. "I've been saving for years, but it turns out I don't need as much as I thought I did." He stuffed some bills into Marco's shirt pocket. "Don't wait until you're my age to spend it."

As Evie wandered along the storefronts, Ford followed her, twenty paces behind. In front of several shops she stopped and peered into the glass and he wished he were close enough to see what had caught her eye. One storekeeper erupted from the doorway, his hands gesturing while his lips moved in time, though Ford was too far away to hear. Evie nodded, almost a bow, and stepped inside, only to emerge minutes later empty-handed. She waved to the blank doorframe. At the end of the next block she stopped and glanced back in Ford's direction as if she weren't sure whether he was coming or not. He hurried to catch up.

"What did he want?" he asked.

"Who?"

"The man who ran the hardware store."

"He had a new shipment of canvas bags."

"You didn't buy one."

"Nope, don't need a canvas bag." She took his hand and swung it as she walked. "How about you?"

"Nope, I don't need a canvas bag either. Breakfast, though, that would be good."

"We should have bought fish and taken it back to the motel and grilled it on the stone barbecue out by the pool. Do you think everyone up here eats fish for breakfast?"

"I'll bet the families of the dock boys do."

During breakfast at a shingled harborside restaurant, Ford was careful not to mention mothers or fathers, even though the photo of his dancing parents hovered in black and white in the shadows. He didn't want to spoil the day by starting with an argument, and he wasn't ready to tell Evie that he had decided to go back. The trip had been planned as discovery and he hated to lose a minute getting to know this woman. Outside the restaurant when Evie stopped to admire a baby in a stroller, he hung back.

The soft indistinguishable conversation between Evie and the mother washed over him along with the snapping sound of line against mast, waves lapping at the stone pier, and random shouts from the nearby boatyards. The morning sunlight clutched at rooflines and treetops as if it weren't ready for full-blown midday glare either. Gently it touched the corner of the stroller and the tops of the women's dark heads where they bent to discuss the baby. Without any schedule the day stretched ahead of them. They were together. Life was good.

Evie was grinning when she stood back up and waved good-bye to the mother. "Did you see that baby smile? Kids are so great. They live on this simple plane of eating and sleeping. Any little bit of stimulation and they smile or cry and someone answers them. Life as a baby, what a dream."

"I thought your sister didn't have any children."

She strode off without waiting for him. The abruptness surprised him. Since she'd brought up the topic of children, he'd been prepared to talk about it. This sudden feeling of separation from her and from all women filled him with foreboding. Children, and all the issues surrounding them, symbolized innate feminine emotions men claimed not to understand. It was the same gap that had made it impossible for him to keep up with the women he'd dated, a chasm of miscommunication. Odd how he'd never noticed it in his mother until he began to see her as more than merely his mother.

Over the centuries men had built an enormous mountain between themselves and women, an obstacle to empathy, an obstacle to celebration of their differences, an obstacle to love that lasted beyond sexual desire. He stood at the base of that mountain. Envisioning the climb, he wondered how he could possibly succeed where millions had failed. Even worse, genetically he was doomed. His own father had run away rather than work at it.

Here was proof of the mountain. When he expressed interest in a subject she raised, she cut him off without giving him a clue. In light of her withdrawal, his imagination carried forth its own conversation, the possibilities rendering him speechless as well. Was her sister divorced? Did she have a child who died of some horrible disease?

When he caught up with Evie, he put his arm around her shoulder. "Sorry. I didn't mean to make you uncomfortable."

Although she slowed enough to let his arm rest there, she didn't look at him or answer. When she spoke it was edged with sadness. "Why do you always apologize? You're not the only one who makes mistakes, you know."

A new apology shriveled on his lips. Quelling the urge to squeeze her closer, he let his arm drop and walked on in a concerted effort to stop the spin of possibilities in his mind. She must regret coming, he was such an inarticulate clod. He couldn't even apologize right.

At a break between houses, the ocean came back into sight. A narrow strip of stone beach was wedged between two larger groups of rocks, darkened with algae and barnacles and iron. The green water rushed in, shoving aside the tentacles of brown seaweed to reach the shallow pools on the topmost rocks. The water and noise, in a panting rhythm, rose and receded. He stood on the concrete sidewalk above the rocks and let the salt spray fall on his arms and face. That long-ago day when his mother had taken him as a boy to the ocean, they had counted waves together. She had told him a story of King Neptune and his adventures. The story had ended with Neptune's unsuccessful search for the perfect Queen, how every seventh wave was big, an everlasting reminder that there were lots of possibilities and they were all hard to hold onto. It was one of the few fairy tales he could remember his mother sharing.

Several minutes passed before Evie reappeared. With one foot on the metal bar of the fence, she leaned against the rail without touching him. He felt the distance between them. Felt her slipping away, racing out with the current. A thousand words surged into his brain, but he couldn't conform his lips to his thoughts. Although he wanted to let her know he understood there were things she wasn't ready to share, he was afraid to say the wrong thing so he didn't say anything at all.

When a kid raced by on a skateboard, just missing their heels, Ford instinctively pulled Evie sideways to avoid injury. She worked at a smile—slight—but a smile all the same. He smiled back. It was enough to bring her back from wherever she'd gone.

"Family is a touchy subject for me," she said. "My sister had an abortion at fifteen. She almost bled to death. She can never have children." While he watched, the green of the ocean glimmered under the dusky green of her eyes. He had an inkling of what she was feeling, but no idea where she was headed.

"My father . . . my father arranged it all. A secret, of course. He didn't want my mother to know."

"Society forced people to hide it back then."

"Oh, no, it wasn't that. My father didn't give a damn about social conventions."

"Evie, we don't have to talk about this. Fathers aren't my favorite subject either."

"I need to tell you this. I go on and on about how you should make up with your father, but I'm not the one to talk with about forgiveness. I gave up on my father years ago. "

"Maybe it was deserved."

"Yeah." She resumed her stance at the rail, staring out at the ocean.

"You can't blame yourself for what your father did. Or didn't do."

"I can. I never even knew what he was doing until after Lucy was gone. For weeks she was on the streets. I couldn't find her."

"Your mother didn't call the police?"

"And say what? That she was married to a man who had raped her daughter? He'd convinced Mom she was the one with the problem. He'd give her a sleeping pill, and then he'd get up from her bed and go in to my sister's. Until she got pregnant. Then he paid the butcher and sent her packing. Damaged goods."

"How did you find her?"

"She found me. She left a note one day in my book bag at school. Told me to get out, that sooner or later he would come looking for me."

The bottom of Ford's stomach fell away. Evie had painted a picture, crystal clear in its inevitability. She'd been the younger sister. And the younger sister would be next. Three years difference, she'd said in an earlier conversation.

With his fingers under her chin, he turned her face to his. "You don't have to tell me any more. I love you." There he'd said it right out. He hadn't thought about it, hadn't planned it. The words had just come. "I love you just the way you are. You are the most wonderful human being I've ever met."

"You're so wrong. I'm flawed like everyone else."

He touched her cheeks where the tears ran down. "Oh, Evie.

All this time I've been obsessing about my family. And I dragged you to bury my mother when the last thing you wanted was more family skeletons."

"I'm just so tired of the lies. I can't do it anymore."

"You didn't lie to me. You never mentioned your family. I pushed. I should have let you tell it when you were ready."

Crying steadily now, she brushed the tears off her face impatiently with the side of her palm. "I left before he . . ."

"Whatever he did is over. You don't need to explain. Our life started two months ago when you came looking for a key."

She smiled through the tears, but still held herself apart. Although what he wanted was to gather her in his arms, he sensed that she was struggling to distinguish her feelings for him as a man with the resentment and disappointment she felt over her father. He gave her some time to pull herself together.

When an old woman wheeled toward them with her groceries rolling along behind in a metal cart, they were forced to separate. The woman's knotted fingers clung to the handle bar as she dragged the cart behind her. Ford thought of his mother's hands, so still in her lap with the single daisy the day he'd brought the photographs. She'd loved flowers, arranged them, bought paintings of them, jammed the window ledges with pots and vases. As if by surrounding herself with living things she could celebrate a world that blossomed anew while she remained the same. Stifled and bitter, she'd missed out on years of pleasure. That choice had cost her more than she'd needed to lose over a husband's desertion. Ford wasn't going to let that happen to him or Evie.

"Beautiful day," the old woman muttered, her head down and her shoulders hunched forward to maintain her momentum.

"Isn't it?" Ford agreed, watching Evie's face to see if she saw the humor in the platitude. While the crooked woman bumped the cart down the curb and limped across to the side street, he stood inches from Evie and memorized her face. Like a charcoal sketch, tiny lines curved around her mouth where she held her lips together while she thought. Her hair curled in wisps by her ears and cheeks. It made her look even younger than she was. Her green eyes followed the roll of the waves, shifting in and back to the same phrase and beat. If the ocean would be quiet, he was sure he would hear her heart pulsing and her lungs shift up and out under her ribs.

After the old woman had disappeared, but the cart still sounded its rattle in the distance, Evie put her hands on the rail again and faced him, sighing. To Ford, it signaled relief that the tears were done.

He smoothed her hair. "Salem's not far. Think you're ready for an afternoon of five-masted schooners and Far Eastern spice traders?"

"I thought Salem was famous for witches."

"There is a dark side to you, Evie Newton, a very dark side."

"So now you know. Have you changed your mind?"

"About what?"

She hesitated as if she were afraid to say the words out loud. It surprised him, but he understood now it wasn't anything he'd said. Her father had done this to her.

"About loving me?" she asked.

"Fat chance."

Chapter Eleven

*A*fter a wild escape through a junkyard on the far side of the burning warehouse, the boys maneuvered Rhue down the subway escalator and onto the first car. They changed directions several times until they were sure no one was following them. No one talked. Rip dug in his pockets until he fished out his note from the library payphone with the address Ford's apartment superintendent had given them. But when Rhue explained the boys didn't need to accompany him, they spouted a list of objections to his taking a taxi. And more objections to his offer to give them money for a ride to school.

"Safer underground," Wizard explained.

"If you haven't done anything wrong, you shouldn't act guilty."

"All it takes is one person who saw the three of us going into that warehouse. Cops don't tend to believe people like us."

"They would if you didn't skip school."

"Listen to that. Fatherly advice from the father of the year?"

Rip tippled the metal trash can by the subway map, and it rocked in place for several long seconds. "You wanna get to your son's place or not?"

"I made it from Montana. I can probably figure out how to get across town."

"Sorry, man." Wizard clapped one hand on Rhue's shoulder in apology. Like a carnival fun house the idling subway car window elongated their reflections. The three gloomy faces could have been brothers, their features so neutralized by the angle and poor lighting. Gone was the excitement of the Internet sleuthing and the rush of escaping the fire.

"Figured out what you're going to say?" Rip pushed. When Rhue didn't answer, he said, "It's gotta be something really good. You took a hike. Like forever. If I were your kid, I'd take that personally."

"I'm open to suggestions."

"No garbage about finding yourself or needing space. That's a cop-out. You gotta tell the truth. Tell him you were scared."

It had never occurred to Rhue. In all the time he'd pursued what he thought were abiding dreams, a grander philosophy of life, he'd not once considered that the dreams were an excuse. If the dreams were false, what else about himself might not be true?

With Rip's scribbled address and the rumpled copy of Adriana's recent obituary in his pocket, Rhue boarded the taxi. Through the rear window he watched the boys depart. After they high-fived each other, they spun on the balls of their feet and disappeared into the crowd. He could imagine Rip performing for friends on a city stoop somewhere. He would mimic the old cowboy's gimpy leg, while the other boys heckled, fascinated all the same. Wizard would recreate the background noises; the crash in the phone booth, the slurp of the wet money in Rhue's cast, the uneven slap of the single boot, and the tap dance on the library floor. The last of their boyhood, about to become men, they had a new story to tell, a small chapter to be added to a lifetime.

They had come to the rescue of a cowboy who had limped into their town, in search of something. To their surprise and his, he had followed them, had listened, and let them teach him. Funny how easy it was when it had been so hard for him to put up with the ranch hands trying to tell him things. If he were to describe Wizard and Rip to the Montana crew, they would never buy it, certain they knew Rhue Hogan as well as anyone. Why had it taken him all these years to realize people could change?

Braced against the stone balustrade outside Ford's apartment building, Rhue pushed the buzzer marked F. Hogan. No answering beep, no human voice. He rang again. The third time he tried the button marked "Super."

"Maurice, here. What'd'ya need?"

"I'm the man who called you about Ford Hogan."

"The man about who?"

"Ford Hogan, one of your tenants. We talked on the phone. I explained I'm visiting from Montana?"

"Man on the phone?"

"Ford's father." He said it more loudly than he'd meant to, but it came out so naturally. At its echo inside the speaker box, he grinned.

"Ford's father? Oh, Ford's father. He's away."

"You said you were going to call him. I thought I might wait here."

"Oh, yeah, yeah, I did call him. He's in Massachusetts, Connecticut, somewhere up there. With Evie. Great girl. You'll like her."

"So ... could you let me in?"

"Jeez, that's so against the rules."

"Look, if you come down, you'll see how harmless I am."

Maurice came out in a jogging suit two sizes too small, a thin stripe of bare belly showing between. He thrust an open bag of chips at Rhue. "Whoa. You two look so alike. The definition of spitting image."

It was a gift Rhue hadn't expected. "Thank you."

"Hah, never said either of you was particularly good-looking." But he shrugged and motioned for Rhue to follow him. "The key's in my apartment. I don't usually keep tenants' keys, but he asked me to ... hey," Maurice stopped abruptly in the middle of the foyer and turned back to face Rhue, the mailboxes lined up on the wall behind him like a Greek chorus. " That cast wouldn't get in the way of watering the plants up there, would it?"

With the key in hand Rhue rode up to the second floor by himself. His heart lurched in the stuffy elevator. Despite his exhaustion, he had been ignoring the tightness, but this pain was sharper. Clutching the wall, he berated himself for not bringing the medicine from the hospital. A lifetime of having only himself to think about had him at a real disadvantage. His first thought was the waste of all this effort if he died on Ford's doorstep. But as the elevator carried him upwards, he saw it from Ford's point of view for the first time.

Leaving the hospital without the complete diagnosis and heading to New York without any plan, those were the actions of an immature person, a selfish person. Ford knew now that his father existed, and that raised expectations. Expectations that it was Rhue's responsibility to meet. Almost more than his departure forty years ago, his unannounced appearance in questionable health would be harder for a son to handle. Most sons had a lifetime relationship that supported the kind of obligations an ailing parent imposed.

He'd meant to offer Ford something positive, a link to his past that had been missing, not a burden to impose on his future. The elevator doors opened and closed as he pressed against his chest bone and willed his heart to slow. It surprised him when the elevator opened on the foyer with its audience of mailboxes. He pushed the button to go up again. When the key worked in Ford's door, he was surprised at that too. This whole trip had been unreal, so different from what he'd imagined. With sirens whining outside the narrow hallway, Montana's unemotional landscape and steady sameness might have been the mirage.

He sat in Ford's living room in the dark. The air was filled with unfamiliar smells; clove and coffee, perspiration, and stale radiator heat. With his eyes closed, he tried to envision his son in these rooms, selecting a book from the shelves, raising the window shade, padding on bare feet to the kitchen. He tried to imagine his son grown.

He didn't explore the other rooms. Embarrassed to be in Ford's personal space without permission, he'd gone straight to the armchair and had barely changed positions since. Although the couch might give better support for his leg, he didn't move. He needed to conserve energy for Ford's arrival. He wasn't sure his heart could take much more excitement.

Maurice hadn't revealed Ford's schedule—maybe he didn't know—but he had confirmed that Ford knew his father was in the city. When Maurice didn't volunteer Ford's reaction to the announcement, Rhue didn't ask. An absence of forty years hadn't earned him any credits.

From the coffee table Rhue fingered a photo from a pile of scattered snapshots. They were black and whites, curled at the corners, mostly of him and Adriana surrounded by friends. The names wouldn't come back to him. He'd trained himself too well. Even with the beard, it shocked him how young he looked. Ford must have found the photos recently, somehow related to his mother's death. That would explain why they were out, but so disorganized as to time.

Next to the photos was what looked like a handwritten list in neat capital letters, a scientific list, so careful and clinical, made without apparent emotion. After the first glance, Rhue looked away. The list was too intimate. It was almost like looking into his son's mind. These were Ford's personal things. He had not expected his father to appear and inspect them.

Rhue understood the separateness of their lives in spite of the blood connection. For the last forty years he had guarded his own privacy fanatically. Even with Marian and Vince there'd been things he never mentioned. Old habits were hard to break.

He slid the list under the photos but not before he noticed that the question marks had no corresponding answers. He wondered if the list had to do with the photos. Had Adriana died before Ford asked? Or were the answers not to his liking?

While Rhue had often wished for a picture of Ford, it had never crossed his mind that his son might be curious too. Rhue's good memories of his own father were bittersweet. All the arguments when he was still at home about schoolwork and his father's expectations had distanced them. Even though his father had not been happy about Rhue's living with a woman without benefit of marriage, he'd been more disappointed when Rhue left them behind.

During those first few years out West whenever Rhue called his parents, he didn't ask about Adriana and the baby. It avoided the familiar tirade about his irresponsibility. He guessed his father, a stickler for social protocol, had stayed in touch with her. At the least he would have insisted on regular meetings with his grandson.

But his father had never volunteered any information. Not long afterward, he'd died, and Rhue's mother followed a few months later. The opportunity was lost.

In the quiet apartment Rhue began to compose mental answers to questions he imagined would be on any son's list. As he sat and looked at the young Adriana and Rhue, he saw in her expression things he'd missed back then: the easy way she linked arms, her smile above the heads of the others. He had never noticed that appreciation, her admiration for him. He'd accused her of lying to him, of only pretending to be strong, of using the hackneyed expectations of society to shame him into staying to avoid her own embarrassment at losing a husband.

He'd rebelled against those expectations, but in the rebellion he'd missed what showed in all the photos, how much she loved him. The puzzle of how to preserve himself, faced with her plans for them, had stumped him. And flailing wildly to free himself, he'd lost the opportunities that love extends.

Waiting here for Ford, he realized he could fail all over again. Disappointment and resentment, building consciously or subconsciously, would create a rift beyond imagination. It had taken Rhue forty years to come back and face them, and yet he was asking Ford to bypass a lifetime of disappointment in the single day it took to drive back from New England. How could there be enough between them in mere genetics to get around those forty years? He would have to convince Ford love meant something to him when he'd rejected it so wholeheartedly with Adriana. The photos revealed a truth he hadn't taken the time to consider in his rush to escape Vince's fate.

With a hollow place in his stomach he watched the sun set. The room fell into a static dimension where time and place meant nothing. This world without Adriana was new to him. In all his years in the hills, riding ponies, fording rivers, camping under stars, she'd been on the other side of the continent; doing the things he remembered her doing and winding that hair into neat twists of midnight ebony. He hadn't realized how much he'd relied on the idea that she existed in the old world exactly as he'd left her. Silly, really, for all he'd known she could have been dead, or remarried, or so broken-hearted she'd withered into someone he wouldn't have recognized on the street.

He took out the obituary and reread it. It didn't say how she died. He imagined an accident, a car crashing into a pedestrian, her body airborne, the shadow toppling as the body fell beneath spinning wheels. Or a frozen gesture, eyes beseeching as her heart stopped suddenly in mid-sentence. No matter what had happened, it must have been a shock for Ford to lose his only parent.

The microfiche newspaper article listed her accomplishments and honors. Some Rhue must have known back when they were together, but they all sounded foreign and impressive here, displayed in two inches of expensive typesetter's ink. In that regard Ford had been lucky to have those years with his mother. "Survived by her son, Ford Simmons Hogan, also of New York." the paper read. No recitation of a daughter-in-law or grandchildren.

Rhue's own obituary would be short. No one knew how he'd lived. Only the horses remembered him. He had been a member of no groups, had chaired no committees, had raised no funds for charities. And he could hardly claim his son.

Every so often there were footsteps in the hallway outside the apartment. The elevator doors glided open and shut in a mechanical whisper. Waking from half-sleep each time, Rhue held his breath, but the steps never stopped at Ford's door. Flustered by the apartment manager's fuzzy welcome earlier, Rhue couldn't recall much of their brief conversation in the downstairs hallway. Maurice obviously didn't know Ford well enough to know he'd never met his father, because he'd treated Rhue like family. The questions Rhue had wanted to ask weighed down his brain so that when a break came in the fellow's running monologue, he was so deep in thought, he only asked if he might wait upstairs.

It wasn't until the elevator stopped running, and the building noises died, that he remembered the duffle. When he telephoned the station though, the man in charge was on break. They suggested he call back in the morning. He'd forgotten what the sign said about storage limits. The longer he sat and thought about what he would say to his son, the less he cared about the duffle or the money.

He wondered why he'd brought it at all. What had he been thinking? That he would move here permanently, welcomed or feted for doing the right thing finally, maybe even reunited with Adriana. The money could hardly serve as reparation for the years of absence. Even the decision to save the money all those years seemed suspect now that he was here, so close to what he'd really come for, not for forgiveness, but to know this son who would live beyond him, who would own the future he would never see. A way to cheat death, was that his real motivation?

Through the gloom he read the titles of the books on the shelves. Mostly classics, Hemingway and Conrad, a fair amount of poetry, a few biographies. On the bottom shelves, dusty and jammed together, thicker books on chemistry and genetics crowded out piles of magazines, stored sideways. Ford the scientist had a humanist's passions. It was not unexpected. Adriana's son would be well educated.

Even with the stupor of interrupted sleep, the hasty departure, and the awkwardness of dragging the cast around the city and out of the burning warehouse, Rhue's mind churned, unable to let go of the uncertainty he'd stirred up by coming here. He imagined two dark heads together at the window. Without having been there, he knew she had read to Ford, as a baby and as a little boy. She would have instilled her love of words in her son in the same way she had enticed her lover Rhue to live with her. Smiling in spite of himself, he recalled the lyrical voice, the bold smile, the pale fingers turning the pages. He remembered leaning closer to hear.

All the miserable silent hours they'd spent at the end and the unspoken words rushed back at him as he sat here in this strange room. The streetlights cast irregular bars of light on the furniture and walls. Imprisoned in the dark, he was sorry he had missed her. He would never know whether she had forgiven him or not. He'd come too late for that.

Yet despite that weight of sadness, he felt hopeful. It might be easier for Ford, without her disapproving presence, to let something happen between them. If Ford would just give him a chance to explain, he would . . . what would he do? Give his son back the years he'd lost? Share stories and photos of Ford doing things that he, as his father, should have been there to see?

All old men have regrets, he lectured himself. Don't lose

perspective. His experiences made him the kind of man he was, and Ford's had shaped him. Just because they'd lived separate lives didn't mean they had nothing in common. Maybe Ford climbed mountains or raced cars. Maybe in his laboratory work he challenged scientific boundaries. They had the same genes, which had to mean something.

From the apartment manager's conversation, it sounded as if Ford hadn't rejected the possibility of reconciliation. Although Maurice hadn't said one way or the other that Ford was definitely on his way back, Rhue conceded that he would need some time to adjust to the idea. Anyone would.

Out of the blue he recalled Maurice's sheepish request for him to water the plants, *as long as you're up there.* Scrounging under the kitchen sink, he found a plastic watering can and made the rounds. He needed sleep but was uncomfortable usurping space that wasn't his. He tried one of the books, a biography of Teddy Roosevelt but wasn't able to concentrate. He replaced it with care, sure from the apartment's organized state that his son paid attention to things like that.

Rhue considered the windows opposite Ford's and the people who lived behind them. Were there other men who had chosen to stay with wives and children, but who were awake at three in the morning, wishing they'd gone west? He could tell them things about the weight of loneliness, the sounds of guilt.

When his legs twitched with restlessness, he hobbled around the room, placing the cast down gently so as not to disturb the tenants below. It had been a long while since he'd worried about neighbors. Several times on the trail Marian and Vince and he had been boisterous enough to rile the other trail riders. A good campfire was something he didn't like to waste. With the coffee cooling almost as quickly as it was poured into their tin mugs, Marian would convince Vince to tell a story. Then they'd lean back against their saddles and listen to his voice rise and fall across the embers.

When Vince was stringing one of his tall tales, Marian would tease him about the steers always ending up noses to the fire. Vince's stories were pure fabrication, but it was impossible not to hang on every word. He had a rare talent to be able to create a world with words that would hold your attention when your body was so tired you couldn't stand up to chase off the coyotes. Vince turned the everyday into the fantastic. The problem with his version of life, though, was that an ordinary person couldn't survive in that world. Someone had to get up in the morning to light the fire or there wouldn't be coffee.

Sitting in the dark apartment remembering the prairie, Rhue recognized his own sense of order in his son's space. These three small rooms existed with minimal intrusion on the outside world. The books were arranged by categories. There were two chairs at the table, not four. Each piece of furniture was bare, without decoration. Except for the loose photographs, the rooms could belong to anyone. No newspapers, folded open or otherwise. No half-drunk glass of water. No sweatshirt tossed over the back of a chair. It almost seemed as if Ford had been biding his time also.

After Rhue had left Adriana and New York, he'd made a point of taking up the smallest amount of space he could. In the places he chose the horizon always stretched out before him, preserving his ability to escape. It had started with his father's rigid view of what counted in this world, complicated by Adriana's demands and the starched-shirt job. Whenever ranchers asked him to stay on after a cattle drive, he said no. He might show up for their next ride, but he refused to promise. Some bosses understood the distinction and didn't press him. The ones who tried to persuade him to commit in advance never saw him again.

Even with those Rocky Mountain winters staring him down with their sure dearth of work, he had refused to obligate himself to anyone or anything. Vince and Marian never questioned it. When the three of them finished a job, they never talked about what they were going to do with their earnings or where they were headed. It always made him laugh when Vince walked into the same bar where he'd landed, or when Marian strode into the same casino, her pockets heavy with money she was anxious to get rid of. With all their talk, they were creatures of habit. They conformed to a norm they set themselves while they denied its existence in the same breath.

After New York, he'd avoided making promises. He lived alone. He moved a lot. Even with Marian who touched him once or twice in the early days as if she wanted more, he'd kept himself apart. What had he been afraid of, that she might demand something from him he couldn't give? Or that he wouldn't be able to live up to her expectations? If Ford had inherited those fears, he might have made the same mistakes, might still be making them.

When the tenants began to stir in the morning and the elevator whizzed into action, Rhue panicked. He wasn't ready to talk to Ford after all. He needed more time and a shower. Standing in the Spartan kitchen, he used the phone on the wall. The hotels with ads in the yellow pages were full or unable to give him a reservation without a credit card, something he'd never needed on the trail. After a dozen strikeouts with addresses he recognized, he decided he'd have to go out and find a place in person. He was hungry too. Ford's refrigerator was as good as empty. The shelf over the stove revealed unopened tuna fish and canned peaches.

On a pad by the phone he wrote a note. "Had to arrange for my luggage. Back about seven p.m." Although he signed it "Rhue Hogan," he hoped he'd be back in time to destroy it before Ford read it and found significance in the use of a stranger's name. A note instead of a live person would only exacerbate old doubts.

Just as he was leaving the phone rang. He froze and listened to it ring. As much as he didn't want their first conversation to be on the telephone, it might be Ford calling to alert him to his arrival. After a dozen rings Rhue answered.

"Is this the cowboy?" Wizard's voice bit into the words like a drill sergeant, but the lingering buzz was pure panic.

"Wizard?"

"They let us make one phone call."

"The police?"

"Yeah. We been here all night. They think we lit the frigging fire."

"Which station house?"

Although he'd been daydreaming about waffles and bacon, his appetite disappeared. He grabbed one of the old photographs of himself with Adriana. If the police were to put any weight in his crazy explanation, his link to someone real in the city would have to be made crystal clear. A homeless stranger and two juvenile delinquents would make easy scapegoats for overworked detectives. Nonexistent fathers were hard enough. But behind bars, a wandering cowboy wouldn't even get an audience.

Maurice came to his door in a bathrobe, but was awake enough to offer coffee. After Rhue refused, the man leaped right into a gripping summary of the Yankees' doubleheader, somehow connected to Rhue's being a visitor to New York.

Rhue cut him off by handing him Ford's key. "Something's come up. But I'll be back."

The taxi delivered him to the Madison Square Garden side of the train station. Although he didn't really want to lug the duffle around with him, he wasn't sure how police in the city did business and cash might help, to post bond or otherwise. He rode the escalator down to Left Luggage, surrounded by bigger-than-life-size advertisements of sports stars and actresses. As they stared back at him, he felt the sense of déjà vu that World War II heroes described when they returned home after being in Europe for a year or two. Home seemed less familiar than the foreign country because their experiences overseas had been so intense. In the last four days he had lived a lifetime and relived part of another.

He limped hurriedly past food stalls and travelers sitting on their suitcases. Anxious policemen wouldn't wait forever for some mystery man to appear with an alibi before they took the boys before the magistrate, charged them, and sent them off to detention. Not that he was the best reference in the world, but he had no criminal record. His ancient Yale degree could be verified. The money might make a difference.

Behind the Left Luggage desk the uniformed man in charge simply put out his hand, palm up. Rhue felt in his jacket pocket for the ticket. The woman behind him coughed. Ignoring her, he continued to search. When she coughed a second time, he moved aside and kept searching. The receipt wasn't in any of his jean pockets or in his shirt pocket either. Although he checked each pocket twice, he thought he remembered putting it in his right hand jacket pocket before he'd left the counter. The only other thing he'd carried in the jacket was his water bottle and that had been in the left pocket. He hadn't taken off the coat at all.

Once he and the attendant were alone again, Rhue stood foursquare in front of the counter. "Look, I've been all over this city in the last twenty-four hours. That ticket could be anywhere. If I can describe the bag and the contents, can't you just make an exception? No one else could tell you what's in it." He didn't wait for an answer. "It's a dark green duffle, faded badly, with two pieces of clothesline around it—old clothesline—about eight inches from each end. I don't know the manufacturer, but it's four feet long. Approximately. Inside—"

"Rule's the rule, bud. Find the ticket or the bag stays put."

"That rule was intended to protect owners. I can prove the

bag is mine. There's a T-shirt in it from the Calgary Stampede. Who else would know that?"

"Look," the attendant pointed to the people who had collected again behind Rhue. "If I were to give out suitcases to every Joe who came through here claiming he'd left one, I'da been fired years ago. I got a month to retirement and I'm not giving up a bag without a ticket. Move aside, Mister."

Rhue went to the closest restroom. In the stall he took out the plastic bag of cash from the cast to see if he'd stuck the ticket there for some reason. No luck. The good-bye scene with the boys came back to him. Although Wizard had hung back, Rip had hugged him. He could have taken the ticket then. It didn't make much sense—they'd had several chances to hit him over the head and take everything—they knew he had no wallet and they'd seen the one hundred dollar bill come out of the cast. But it was also logical for them to figure out he'd brought luggage if he'd come all the way from Montana.

He wiped his palms on his jeans. If the warehouse fire was part of a sting, it was oddly coincidental how the boys had arrived in the nick of time. Was he being taken all over again with the alibi request? A trick to produce a real suspect for the police?

The hour of story-telling in the warehouse rushed in on him. The boys had seemed genuinely interested. His instincts, even in the city, couldn't be that off. The police would be anxious to process someone, and the boys had already been detained overnight.

He went back and waited in line again. When he reached the counter, he smiled at the luggage check man. He laid a twenty dollar bill on the counter, his body between the money and the other customers. "Could you at least do me a favor and look and tell me whether my bag is still back there? Someone may have taken my ticket."

"Stolen it?" The smack of the attendant's gum resounded more when it wasn't repeated. The twenty dollar bill slid over the edge of the counter and out of sight.

Rhue paused, feeling disloyal for even thinking it. "Maybe." All he wanted was to retrieve the bag, straighten out this glitch for the boys—he owed them—and get back to the apartment. After coming all this way, not being there when Ford arrived would not be a good beginning. The clerk stared at him so long that Rhue looked down to see if he'd spilled something on his shirt.

After the man rifled through a stack of papers, he handed one to Rhue. "If your ticket's been stolen, you fill out this report. If you can identify the luggage and the contents, Regulation 293 says I can give you the bag." But before Rhue could thank him, he added, "It usually takes twenty-four hours. For the clearance on the report. And, if the bag's already gone, we aren't responsible."

At the precinct the desk officer analyzed the ten-gallon hat, the single boot, and Rhue's bare toes. Without speaking, he went back to his paperwork. Rhue started again, reciting the boys' phone call and their chance meeting two days before. During the recitation the policeman didn't look up once.

Head still buried in paperwork, he finally interrupted Rhue's monologue. "If you aren't related or the attorney, I'm not allowed to let you in."

"Could I speak with Rip or Wizard by telephone?"

"The prisoners?"

"They're just being detained for questioning. I think."

"Those their real names?"

Rhue was beginning to lose hope. "Couldn't I talk with the detective in charge?"

"Maybe."

"Will you ask him?"

"Her."

Rhue leaned his elbows against the raised desk front. He hadn't slept enough, though his chest didn't ache at the moment. The time since Wizard's phone call had raced past. It was almost noon. The cast, splayed sideways to avoid pressure on the open sore, stuck into the narrow passageway. Every time someone passed, he had to slide it in closer to his body, which jammed the plaster into the blister. He still needed a shower, badly. He could feel his blood pressure rising.

Behind him a woman broadcast her complaint over his shoulder at the desk officer. From what Rhue understood of the broken English, she'd been robbed. She listed the missing items. He thought he heard cat food. When the policeman lowered his head and winked where the woman couldn't see, Rhue grinned back. She made even a traveling cowboy look sane.

Rhue cleared his throat when the woman took a breath. "Were you going to ask the detective anytime today?" he asked.

The sergeant said nothing, but he picked up the phone as

he motioned for Rhue to take a seat. Although the line of visitors had waxed and waned in spots, the crazy woman held her ground. She kept right on with her complaints and her list; twisting in place to whomever was closest for an audience.

"Mr. Hogan." The desk sergeant replaced the receiver without changing his facial expression. "Detective Long says you can come back. Second door on your right, down the corridor, turn left at the water fountain. She'll meet you at the stairs."

Rhue groaned at the thought of more stairs. When he tried to swing his leg around, the woman who'd been robbed still didn't move. Although they stared eye to eye, she didn't budge. Finally he tipped his hat and she stepped back. He wove his way down the hallway between clumps of people, some in business suits—defense lawyers, he assumed—and some in the eclectic costumes he associated with New York.

Behind a door with a glazed window he spotted two shapes that could be the boys, huddled together as they had for the street conferences. When the door opened and a woman in a business suit streamed out, her briefcase swinging aggressively ahead of her, Rhue saw two derelicts, their clothes stained and their voices guttural and slurred. They had at least two decades on Rip and Wizard. His relief was instant, even with half a day wasted and his mind playing tricks on him.

Before the door swung shut, while he was still focused inside, a woman with a legal pad careened around the corner and ran right into him. Knocked off balance, he stumbled sideways and ended up on the floor with his back against the water cooler.

"Oh, God, I'm so sorry." She dropped the pad and leaned

over to help him. Her pen rolled under the radiator. "I didn't expect anyone to be right there." Hesitant about where to put her hands, she continued to apologize. "Are you all right? My luck, you're probably a disabled veteran on the undercover handicapped patrol."

Rhue laughed and grabbed her extended hand. Using the radiator as additional leverage, he yanked himself back to upright. She was still staring at the cast.

"It was already broken," he explained.

While she didn't laugh, she batted at him awkwardly, smoothing his shirt and adjusting his collar. He introduced himself as the reference for Rip and Wizard. She paused to examine his face. She was actually smiling for the first time. "You're the man that Richard Isaiah Porter and Wesley Morgantown were talking about?"

Choking back his surprise at their given names, he nodded. "Have they been charged?"

"No, just present in the wrong place at the wrong time. Arson's suspected, but so far no real evidence. My patrolmen are a little overzealous. Their collective wisdom is all street kids must be punks. And in this case Wesley's dad is a three-time felon."

"Which translates into an automatic arrest for the son? That seems like a stretch, even for an overworked city cop."

"The old man could be dragging his kid into stuff like this."

"Stuff like this?"

"Insurance fraud."

She picked up the pad and slipped into an adjoining office,

pulling drawers open and feeling inside, he assumed for another pen. He waited in the open door.

"Anyway," she moved in front of him and motioned down the hallway, "it never hurts to keep the juvies a little scared. Amazing how that keeps them out of trouble and cuts down on my caseload. What'd you say your name was?"

"Rhue Hogan."

"Address, occupation?" The new pen hovered above the page.

"Retired horse trainer. Vacationing from Montana."

"In New York City?" She shook her head back and forth as if she'd heard everything now.

"I used to live here." At her continued look of disbelief, he added, "A long time ago."

"You trained horses here?"

"No, worked for Legal Aid. We lived on 82nd Street, west side."

"Identification?"

Although he tried to imply total confidence by staring back for several seconds, he had to lean down to locate the driver's license in the cast.

"Yeah," she waved her hand, "that was a stupid question. I should have known the ID would be in the cast."

Swinging the door of the next room wide, she motioned for him to precede her. He signaled back and she conceded. When she entered, both boys stood up, but, as soon as they saw who was behind her, they moved toward Rhue. She pointed at the chairs and they obeyed.

"Here's your buddy, come to put in a good word for you."

She surveyed their faces while Rhue positioned the cast and lowered himself into one of two empty chairs. Perched across the corner of the table, she let one leg dangle loose. Her one sharp look up at the wall and away was fast enough he thought maybe he'd imagined it, though it made sense they'd have a two-way mirror. Three of them and one of her, no matter how well-trained she was. And they hadn't frisked him either, a lapse that surprised him, though the cast may have distracted them.

She had hiking boots on under her suit pants. "Okay, Wesley, why don't you tell me how you know this gentleman?"

Wizard shrugged in Rhue's direction, a hint of a smile on his lips as if to apologize for the name. "He hired us to help find his . . . uh, someone." The hesitation was not quick enough.

"Someone like who?" Detective Long demanded.

"He can tell you."

"If I want him to tell me, I'll ask him."

Wizard drew his hands into his lap, where the fists twitched, a pointed contrast to the measured emotionless voice. "It's his private business. Ma'am."

The detective jammed the pen onto the side of the pad and slapped it on the table. "I'm impressed. Loyalty among thieves."

Rhue interrupted. "They're just being polite. I was having trouble negotiating the cast with the crowds. The boys offered to help. They did the research and found the person I was looking for. At the library."

"And the connection between the library and the warehouse is—"

Rip hopped up and gestured with both arms. "It's just a place we go to get away from things. It's quiet. No little brothers and sisters. The gangs don't know about it. Sometimes we study there."

Detective Long snickered.

Rip flashed Rhue a look of complete disgust. "Or play cards or sleep. The electrical's been screwy for years."

"You, meaning you and Wesley? Or you and the wandering cowboy?" Her voice was flat, like a recorded prompt.

"Wizard. He's my best friend."

"Sweet," she grimaced at Rhue as if he were on her side.

When she didn't ask another question, Rhue spoke. "I needed to rest and they didn't know I had money for a hotel."

"If you had money, why were you hanging around with them?"

He was thinking, but not fast enough for the lady detective.

She shot back. "Why would a grown man, disabled by a cast, in a city full of predators, follow two unknown punks into a deserted warehouse?"

Rip kicked the table leg, stood and faced off, but Wizard yanked his arm and pointed a thumb in Rhue's direction. Without a word Rip sat back down. The detective nodded for Rhue to answer.

"They hadn't rolled me. And they'd had opportunities. You get a sense about these kinds of things."

"You're a psychic too?"

He was remembering the feeling in his stomach when he'd learned Adriana was dead. Explaining the whole long story to this cynical detective didn't appeal to him, but if it would help the boys—

"With your sixth sense, Mister . . . ah, Hogan, can you tell me whether they lit the fire?"

"No."

"No, they didn't or no, you don't know?"

"They went home."

"They told you they went home."

"They told me they went home," he conceded. "I was asleep. The fire woke me up. When they heard the sirens, they came to check on me. Saved my life. I don't think they would have risked being found on the property if they'd struck the match."

"So you admit they're street savvy."

"It's called survival."

"Why should I believe you? You could be part of their scheme."

When he reached into his pocket for the obituary printed below the Library's heading and the old photograph, the door burst open and two uniformed men grabbed his arms, muscled him against the wall, and jammed on handcuffs. He should have figured there was no funding in a city precinct building for a hidden security system to check for weapons.

The next room smelled worse than any barn he'd slept in. Metal bars on the single window, street grime filmed the glass so thickly you couldn't have seen fireworks through it. He mentally reviewed the abbreviated interview with Detective Long. Stupid, he knew better. Pockets hid weapons, they'd been watching through the two-way. She must have changed her mind about his innocence, or maybe she was just busy checking leads and he didn't seem like anyone important enough to complain about the delay.

At least he was able to think without real interruption. He tried to ignore the sounds further along the corridor, clanging and footsteps and random angry voices, answered by curt responses. *Shut up, goddammit*, and *cut the crap*. It was impossible to tell whether it was inmates or policemen. When no one walked past his door, he figured there was no outlet at the far end. From the slant of the shadows on the floor from the window bars, he calculated it was midafternoon.

If he was under arrest—they'd taken off the cuffs, but confiscated his jacket and made him empty his pockets and the cast—they'd forgotten the regulation phone call. He had no idea who he would call. Tiara? Fat lot of good a reference from a Montana madam would do in an East Coast police precinct, though she did have the title to his truck that proved his residency at least as recently as the renewal date last summer. Or Maurice, the person with whom he'd had the longest conversation since his arrival? After Cecily, who had disappeared like a sprite in fantasyland and wasn't a local herself.

The duffle—if they finally did release it to him with the lost ticket report—could substantiate the details of his departure from Montana by train four days ago. That much cash would look bad, though. Under the circumstances, he could be a paid arsonist. Or worse.

Despite all that, if the police asked him, he would refer them to the baggage check office. The stolen bag report and the timing of its storage would match the train's arrival from Ithaca and points west. No time for him or anyone else to deposit cash there as a payoff.

Surely without any ties here, he couldn't be connected to the owner of the burned building, the logical person to orchestrate a fire for insurance purposes. Closing his eyes against the sounds and smells, he propped his leg up on the extra chair. That felt better. If the boys were clean, he'd end up clean. They were the only intersection of association between him and the warehouse.

He didn't want to think what would happen if the boys were involved in the fire somehow. Or if the police followed up on the newspaper information and telephoned Ford.

Chapter Twelve

*F*ord stood in the ocean up to his knees. To keep the circulation going, he hopped from foot to foot. He yelled out to where Evie was swimming laps beyond the line of breaking waves.

"This water's blue for a reason."

She didn't answer. Maybe she couldn't hear above the roar. Seaweed strands floated several inches below the surface and caught at his ankles annoyingly. Although it made him nervous that she was beyond his hearing, he couldn't bring himself to cross over the breakers and swim to her. She'd warned him not to come if he didn't feel confident. Panic, she said, was the number one cause of drowning.

By the time she returned to the shallow water he was ready for a campfire in spite of the sunshine. "Sadist," he said once he held her hand.

"It's so . . . energizing. I can't remember when I've felt more powerful."

"Aquawoman, faster than a speeding bullet—" he teased.

"By the end of the week you'll be out there with me. A few more sessions in the motel pool—"

"Let's not get carried away. You've avoided the shipbuilding museums and the Puritan village. I think I should get to choose where and how far I swim."

"You said you loved the ocean."

"I do. Fantastic vista, but I didn't remember it so cold."

"That's 'cause you were little when you came with your mom. Children aren't affected by things like that."

"Can I ask you a question?"

She stopped drying herself off and looked up, her expression open. It caught him off guard. He hadn't meant to sound so serious.

He wished he would stop dwelling on his father's reappearance. It gave the guy a kind of significance Ford hated to concede. More than curiosity kept bringing him back to mind though. And knowing that Evie had been forced to divorce herself from her own father gave her a unique perspective on his father's abdication.

"Do you think that your father changed the kind of person you are?" He asked.

"That's a trick question."

"I know."

She wrapped the towel around herself and sat on the dry sand just above the high tide line. Sinking down next to her, he dug his feet in. While she thought, he pushed sand around until only his legs stuck out, no toes, no ankles.

"You don't have to—" he started.

"You're apologizing again. You asked and I'll answer. Just give me a minute. I haven't thought about it before in quite that way."

After he rubbed his palms together to get rid of the sand, he smoothed them on her towel. She leaned over and kissed him. Her lips were salty and cold.

When she spoke, her voice was loud to compete with the surf. "In spite of all your convoluted psychological hang-ups, you are the most honest man I've ever met. Most men blame all their failures on the way their father made them play baseball at ten or the way their mother potty trained them. I've never known a guy who was willing to admit he had the choice to refuse what his parents tried to heap on him."

"My mother was too busy trying to heal herself. She actually did me a favor by letting me grow up on my own. I mean, she did all the expected things. Took me to the science museum, made me do Boy Scouts for a few years, insisted I take dance lessons in high school. She just didn't invest herself in my future." Although the waves had edged up the beach so that any minute one might catch them, he stayed, overcome with the urgency of making her understand. "There's a great freedom in making those choices without parental pressure."

"Maybe she blamed herself for your father leaving. She might have pushed him to be someone he wasn't."

"Whose side are you on?"

"For years after I left home I blamed my father for what he did to Lucy and for forcing me to leave. Every time something bad happened to me, I looked for a dartboard with his picture on it. Lucy was the one who showed me how wrong I was." She dug her toes into the sand until she found his. "When she married Joe, she didn't want a church wedding or even a party. I couldn't understand it. Everyone wanted to help her celebrate."

Evie shivered under the towel. Up and down the beach the wind blew the sand in little eddies wherever it met an obstacle. Sand particles swam in the breeze and collected in his mouth, under his eyelids. Spreading the other towel over her shoulders, he pulled the corner around her and held her close to him.

Her voice was muffled. "My mother argued with Lucy. Marriage was hard enough without a church wedding and God's blessing, blah, blah, blah. Lucy finally lost it. After she finished telling Mother what a fraud she was for letting all those years pass without kicking my father out, she went over, kissed Mother's cheek, and announced that life is just a long series of choices you make."

Evie's face appeared from under the towel. She squinted in the sun, but kept her eyes on his. "Lucy felt God had already blessed them by letting them find each other. A formal ceremony wouldn't have changed any of that. Or how she felt about Dad. We are who we are. Sure, other people's actions can change your life. But you choose how to react. You can let it pull you down or you can leave it behind."

Ford kissed her forehead. "You are very wise for someone so young."

"Not so worried about my dark side now?"

"I'm hoping I'll have a long time to get to know all about you, especially the dark side."

They opted for the Salem Witch House, did the tour with a family of seven girls who oohed and aahhed at all the appropriate places in the tour guide's spiel. Ford and Evie found themselves back on the steamy sidewalk with time for a swim in the motel pool before dinner.

After lobster and blueberry pie, her fingers slid in between his as they walked on the slanted sidewalks of Old Town Marblehead. Where the shutters were open in the houses they passed, she tugged for him to stop long enough for her to stand on tiptoes and peek. Many of the owners had decorated their windowsills with bottles of beach glass or figurines. The colors, miniature kaleidoscopes, sprayed across the walls. Their rugs and armchairs and pianos lay open to view like dollhouses in a museum.

Every time she leaned against him to see better, he breathed in a hint of chlorine from the pool and that same lemony smell that followed her everywhere. Because he wanted the moment to last, he let himself ramble.

"Can't you just imagine the gray-haired lady who sits there every evening in her stiff black dress, her embroidered handkerchief poking out of her sleeve? She reads letters from her sea captain by the fading light."

Evie giggled. "And no doubt, weeps herself to sleep. You, sir, are a hopeless romantic."

"Ouch. It's painful enough to see the sorrow in everything without you making fun of me." But he sensed the discussion was not academic for either of them.

She was still smiling though. "Life is more down to earth than you make out, T. The sun comes up. You go to work. Some days you get 93 percent ground chuck and some days you have to settle for 85 percent."

"Not if you shop the right places."

"There's not enough time in the day to waste doing that. If you want time to watch the sunset, you have to buy your dinner at the store on the way home."

"If that's how you feel, why didn't you marry the doctor guy when he wouldn't give up? Your kids would have all the best opportunities and you'd have time to spend with them instead of working."

"Settling for something isn't being practical. It's being lazy."

When he tried to pull his hand away, she held fast. They stood toe to toe on the sidewalk. He wasn't used to having to defend himself, but she was clearly expecting him to respond. "Or realistic. I've worked the same job for almost twenty years. I'm good at it and I contribute something worthwhile to the world."

She didn't answer right away. In the dusky light he couldn't see her eyes. What had started as a joke had turned more serious. He forced a smile. "Plus the hours suit me. And the vacations . . . "

"But," she hesitated, "you mourn for things you never had, instead of enjoying what you have."

"This is still about my father, isn't it? You think I should talk to him." He could feel her hand squeeze tighter as if she were afraid he would slip loose and get away. "I can't help it if the guy cut and ran. Every day I lived with the sadness in my mother's eyes when the phone rang and it wasn't him." He pulled his hand free. "I went to ballgames and school plays, forever scanning the audience, hoping he would be there to see what I was doing. Prayed at night for him to come home. Celebrated her birthdays when I knew she was wishing for him instead of me. It's not so easy to put that behind you."

"Do you think he did it to be hurtful?"

"That's not how she talked about it. But it did hurt her. So, why the hell should I forgive him? Why shouldn't he pay?"

"Oh, I get it. Life is about winning, evening the score, keeping things fair."

"In a way. He chose not to have a son. He chose. Not me. He didn't stick around to change diapers, or help with homework, or take up for me with the debate coach." Although he could hear his voice growing louder and he knew it sounded pitiful, he couldn't stop. "He's old now, probably dying, and he wants to be forgiven. Tough luck. He made his choice."

"But he didn't know you. It wasn't you, Ford Hogan, medical researcher, lover of Eve, dreamer of oceans, he chose to leave."

The easy linking of their names gave him pause, but the old anger flared. "When I needed him, he wasn't there. Why should I be there for him?"

"Because he's asking. Because he's on your way home like the grocery store. Because you have more important things to do."

That caught him off guard.

"I do?"

"Sure. Celebrate us, marry me, make a son of your own and do it right."

"Fine, yes, of course I want those things." He should stop right there. The exact match of her imagined future with his own struck him as so serendipitous that he ought not to risk further discussion. During his hesitation though, a cloud passed over her face. Her eyes dimmed and she ran her fingers through her hair, fretting like a skating coach with a protégé who can't quite spin on her own. Although she'd lauded his honesty, he didn't feel honest now.

The relationship between a man and a woman was more complicated than what she had described. A complex web of emotions and events brought you to a particular point in time and any tiny tear could unravel the web that was your life. The anger and anxiety he'd lived with over his absent father was not something he could let fall away so easily. With all that roiling emotion, he'd muddied the simple perfection of Evie. She stood before him, shrinking as he spoke as if he were hitting her. He wished back the moment from just seconds ago when she'd been peeking into windows. The issue remained; how could he resolve that angry disillusionment, establish a relationship with his father, and still show Evie he would be dependable?

Taking both her hands, he held them against his chest. "What does my father have to do with this minute? Each person has to make his own way. If he taught me one thing, he taught me that. You said it too. This is my life. I won't let his decision ruin things for me. For us."

"Maybe his decision has nothing to do with you." She kissed him, grazing his lips without passion. "What if you discover later you were wrong about your choice not to see him? As wrong as his decision all those years ago. And it's too late, he's dead."

Her face remained still, her lips closed, her hands in his. He watched the veins in her neck where her heart pumped quietly and steadily. He could hear her breathing. In her eyes, wide and deep, he saw the future.

In that vision she sat on a ledge, overlooking the beach. Children's voices rang out from the distance. She smiled at something beyond his sight, and she reached out her hand. He strained to see what it was.

"At least," she said, "if you hear him out, you get to decide."

Suddenly, with the waves flashing, he saw himself. His legs kicked with great vigor and his arms stretched forward. They moved in perfect arched windmills, strong and sure. It wasn't the boat he was swimming for, but the land.

In the sway-backed motel bed they traded funny stories about college and first jobs. She asked about his old girlfriends and teased him about the variety. Making love was a slow, effortless descent to which they gave themselves over, as inevitable an ending to the day as sunrise was to morning. Ford remembered that first moment in his apartment when he'd seen her and his feeling that she had simply arrived late, but where she had meant to arrive all along.

They took their time packing in the morning. Once the decision was made to return to New York, they didn't mention his father again. The idea of losing what they had discovered crystallized into a fragile peace. She held herself aloof. He could tell she recognized his apprehension about the meeting with his father. There were no questions, no jokes, just a quiet comfort in being close without the need to actually touch or talk.

As he imagined the coming reunion, he was struck with how selfish he'd been with her. She'd lost her father too. Perhaps—he was trying to think positively—Rhue would be someone who could offer insights that would ease her burden. There must be something of the man his mother had fallen in love with all those years ago. And forty more years of living had to translate into some kind of wisdom.

Ford didn't say anything, but he watched Evie as she moved about the motel room collecting her things. During the three days they seemed to have appeared by magic on every surface. He took delight in the innocuous way she marked her territory. The beach glass earrings, the nail file, the ragged Reader's Digest splayed open to the joke page, the socks she wore at night to ward off the New England chill: he catalogued them all and stored the images away for a time when he might need a reminder of this moment. It was hard to be so close and not touch her as she passed.

Despite her ownership of the room, she took every chance she had to pause at the window. The odd little elderly couple was gone. What was she looking for in the narrow slice of garden and pool? He wondered if, like him, she was not looking at all, but thinking instead, reviewing the journey, fitting what she'd learned about him into her version of their relationship, the way a puppy worked a blanket until the indentation fit just right.

"Did Maurice say where your father was staying?" she asked after she parked her suitcase next to the door.

"My apartment."

"How d'he get in?"

They looked at each other and laughed. Lazy Maurice. A relief plant waterer, no matter who he said he was, would have been welcomed, feted, given a key. Ford felt thankful. That a small thing like a landlord's laziness could conjure a father at the exact moment when he needed that father seemed miraculous.

In the car Evie sat close to him. He could feel her elbow at his waist. She didn't talk or sleep or sing. Neither of them turned on the radio. He supposed she was thinking of her own parents, what they'd done, and her choices about how to deal with it. After they crossed the state line into Connecticut, she asked him what he knew about his father. He told her about the shirts and the Bible.

"Where has he been living all this time?"

He shook his head. "If Mom knew, she never said, although, when I pushed her, she admitted he called once from out West."

"They were unhappy when they were together?"

"I don't think so. In the pictures they're laughing and holding hands. I guess that's why she was so angry when he left her."

Ford could feel Evie's worry, palpable and expanding, a third person between them on the seat. It was a weird sensation. He wasn't used to someone who knew what he was thinking. And he wasn't used to feeling responsible for someone else's happiness. Like sheet corners on a windy clothesline, her hands fluttered with the handkerchief at her neck. Maybe she wasn't as sure about their return to New York as she'd sounded back at the motel. Before he figured out a way to ask her though, she spoke again.

"At least you never knew him." With one finger she followed the veins in his hand. "I mean, you didn't know what you were missing."

The pain in her voice was personal now. Their discussion had reopened the wound of her own father's deception, adding a bittersweet edge to her attempt to cheer him up. In a way, by working through his own anger out loud, he'd caused this new pain, without meaning to, and he scrambled to think how to ease it. His perspective changed. An absent father seemed less of a loss than one who willfully harmed his child. Then, too, there was Marco, who'd lost his childhood when his father drowned, but had accepted his circumstances and moved beyond the loss. It wasn't solely a question of the passage of time.

"Well, Mom never talked about him, so I had no way of knowing." Ford struggled to show her he was trying to be positive. "Anyone who would do what he did had to be confused. At the very least."

But when he looked at Evie, just for a second because he was driving and he couldn't risk a crash, she wasn't crying. She was grinning.

"Like father, like son?" she said.

After they found the Merritt Parkway, they stopped to telephone Maurice to let him know they were on their way back; Evie's suggestion. He agreed it might relieve some of the building tension that had slowed his driving to the legal minimum.

"Maybe I'll go scout out the grocery store while you two talk," Evie said as they walked to the pay phone behind the gas station.

"Okay," but he still didn't trust himself to keep his temper with his father.

"It will give you a chance to talk without worrying about how I fit into the picture."

He didn't argue, though he hoped he'd never again have to make any decision without considering her part in it. While he fished in his pocket for coins, the sound of the cars headed north to the suburbs drowned out her words, and he gave up trying to converse.

Love, the way his mother had talked about it, could tangle you up as easily as it could offer that chance at eternity. But the way she'd lived it had been just the opposite. She'd been a good parent, interested, available, supportive. Never had she shrunk away from him because he reminded her of the lover who had rejected her. While she had criticized Rhue as a man, she'd never talked irreverently of marriage or love. Maybe it had been Ford's imagination that had made her moods significant, his own craving for his missing father that had colored her sad when she might only have been pensive.

Maurice answered right away, as if he'd been waiting by the phone. "Where are you, man?" he asked. His dog yipped in the background.

"A couple more hours. How's the old man doing?"

"He's gone."

"Don't joke, Maurice." Ford watched Evie's head snap to attention, even ten feet away. "We've driven three hundred miles because you said the guy was waiting for me."

"He was. But he left early this morning."

"Without saying anything?"

"I figured you'd talked to him from the road."

It was logical, exactly what most fathers and sons would have done. There wasn't much else to say.

Although Evie rubbed the back of his neck when they got back in the car, she eyed him warily and didn't ask any questions. Steering back onto the thruway, he let the cars in a hurry speed past. He concentrated on the road signs so he wouldn't miss the connection to the Tappan Zee. In her own world Evie patted the open map on her lap and after a bit, started to hum, "Onward Christian Soldiers."

In spite of himself, he had to laugh. "Okay, I'll tell you the latest, even though it's driving me bananas. He's disappeared again."

"As in left town?"

"Maurice has no idea."

"Are you sure Maurice is getting all this straight?"

"No."

A car honked and he swerved back into his lane. Blinking against the late afternoon glare, he focused on the unbroken white line that marked the edge of the highway. He tried to block out the image of a bearded man turning the street corner and disappearing. The image, there and gone, was replaced by a stream of pedestrians, typical city types, a nanny with a stroller, a woman jogging with her dog, two businessmen deep in conversation. Life went on.

Worried she would think he was despairing, he interrupted his own thoughts. "We could turn around. There's loads of stuff to see in the Hudson River Valley. No ocean, but I bet we could find another swimming pool."

"Whatever you want."

If he hadn't been driving, he would have hugged her for not making out like it was a crisis. "Maybe it wasn't my father at all, but a traveling salesman selling encyclopedias."

"Or an identity thief, who's taken all your plants and started a nursery on 58th and Madison."

"Maybe he got cold feet."

"That runs in the family."

He laughed again, surprised at how easily, after all these years without a father, he was adjusting to having one. "But if it was him . . . and he's depressed . . . or in trouble and I don't at least try to find him . . ." When she smiled back, he made a mental note to kiss her the next time they stopped.

Chapter Thirteen

*A*lthough the jailhouse dinner came in steaming on a plastic tray, Rhue couldn't eat, for imagining it was the same thing they were feeding the inmates. He pushed the tray away and tried to ignore the growls from his stomach. His last meal had been peanut butter and crackers in the warehouse. After he ran water in the corner sink as hot as he could stand, he washed his head and upper body with his handkerchief. He felt the need to be sharp. Hunger helped.

The nights he'd spent in cells were distant memories from his first few cattle drives, a time when he heard a challenge in any stranger's hello. He'd been drinking then to convince himself he'd made the right choice in leaving Adriana. Afterward, hung over, feeling stupid, he'd be released after paying bond to guarantee his appearance before a judge he'd never see again. It hadn't taken him more than a season to see the dead end there. And forty years to recognize the motivation.

Detective Long came back before he finished washing. She'd put on her suit jacket, not a good sign.

"Hogan," she announced as if there were a dozen men waiting in the room with him. "All clear."

"And I was just about to claim my constitutional rights."

"No need. We do have a statement for you to sign."

"The kids?"

"Clear too. Weirdest set of circumstances I've seen in a long time, but it's all verified. Your Montana lease, paid through this month. Your train ticket out here. Your phone bills, with no New York calls for the last six months. The librarian had the sign-in sheet showing the boys were telling the truth about being with you yesterday, and the page you printed there matches the newspaper website."

He was limping along behind her up the rear staircase in the direction of the interrogation room from earlier that day. His leg must be swelling in the cast. It felt like a dead weight and he wondered if he'd cut off the nerves somehow.

"How did you know where to call in Montana?"

"Your girlfriend showed up. She was all worried about your heart."

Trying to hide his surprise, he stopped to readjust the napkins stuffed around the top of the cast. Detective Long didn't wait for him.

"She's a little different. But what the heck? The hat should have tipped me off."

"Tiara's here in New York?"

Long stopped halfway up the stairs and turned to stare at him. "That's not the name she used."

Thoroughly confused, he wondered whom the boys had

sweet-talked into posing as his girlfriend. He wasn't used to such complicated machinations to avoid trouble. Although he felt relief, he wasn't keen either on their resort to dishonesty. He could see the detective was rethinking her decision to release him.

"I've had lots of girlfriends."

She smiled back. "Somehow I knew that. Cecily Blythe ring a bell?"

"Cecily came here?"

"You didn't do right by her, huh?"

He had to laugh, his credibility verified by her assumption that he was a cad as well as potential arsonist. When she laughed too, he realized she'd already moved on to the next possibility.

"Have the boys gone?" he asked when they reached the interrogation room and it was empty.

"No, I'm waiting on signatures from them too."

After Rhue's official witness summary was signed, the detective excused herself. Five o'clock traffic outside the window played like a little boy's birthday party, continuous indistinguishable din punctuated by sudden loud noises. When the door opened, it was Cecily in a double-breasted red suit and a hat with feathers. Detective Long shut the door on them.

Rhue accepted her hug. "Damn. You are good."

"Lots of practice, that's all. Except for the minutest of hesitations when the detective first telephoned."

"She didn't mention that she'd called you. Wonder how–"

"She wanted to know why my card was in your pocket."

"What about your sister?"

"She's gone to a better place."

"I'm so sorry."

"In her sleep. It was the best thing that could have happened. Really. I was on the train platform headed back to Florida when the lady detective caught me on my cell phone. What happened with your son?"

"You can't see that in your crystal ball?"

She took his hand and started to spread the palm wide, but he yanked it away.

"I'm not sure I want to know."

Her hand slid along his sleeve and slipped free as if she knew sympathy did not sit well with him. "You haven't found him yet?"

"He's been away. But he's probably sitting in his apartment right now thinking what a deadbeat his father is for arranging to meet and then not showing up."

"And I'm chatting away as if you had nothing better to do."

"I ought to find Rip and Wizard first."

"Go, go. I have a train to catch."

Her hug was fingertips on his shoulder blades where he'd leaned down to accept the good-bye kiss. Through the station door window, he watched the tallest feather bounce on the top step and sink out of sight.

In the empty waiting room Detective Long took Rhue aside.

"They're minors. I can't release them to anyone except family. And we're having trouble locating anyone who'll admit that."

"List me as a long lost uncle."

"Why do that for them? You wouldn't have been detained but for them dragging you into this."

"There's no magic to being family. Parents aren't automatically good people. They don't always do the right thing by their children. As hard as those two kids are trying to stay away from their fathers' bad habits, can't you show them there's hope?"

"Lie?"

"Just don't shove the odds down their throats."

"I'm not in the business of saving souls."

"Who does it hurt? They aren't criminals."

"Yet."

Insistent on a local address if she was going to bend the rules, she handed him the release forms and he wrote in Ford's apartment with the telephone number. Another thing to explain to his son. While Detective Long went off to tell the boys, Rhue telephoned the apartment. No answer. He couldn't decide if that was good or bad. When Rip and Wizard appeared, the good-byes were harder the second time.

Dragging the cast along the floor to the doorway and out onto the front steps, Rhue led the way this time. The boys trailed after him. When they bunched up on the top step outside the double wooden doors, the shift in balance unsettled him a little. But underneath that, it felt a little like those first times a wild pony had accepted his weight without bucking.

He waited for the patrolmen on shift change to pass before he spoke. "Don't let me be getting calls from police stations all over the city. You were lucky this time."

Wizard gave him a mother-in-law hug, stepping back almost before he leaned in, though the sheepish grin gave him away.

Rip wrapped his arms around Rhue and held fast. To catch his breath, Rhue finally had to push the boy away.

"Don't you guys have somewhere to go?"

Neither boy moved.

"What's the matter? Need a note for the teacher?"

Wizard chuckled. "Cowboy Man, you are too much. Thanks for . . ." he pointed into the police station.

"It only worked because it was the truth."

Swiping at his nose, Rip scuffed at the cement step. "So, are you gonna leave again after you see your kid?"

It took a minute for Rhue to figure out how to answer that. The iceberg's underside had expanded exponentially. Why hadn't he seen it coming? He'd let the boys in, accepted their help, and now they wanted something from him.

Rip was waiting on the top step. His eyes never wavered. "You are gonna see him, aren't you?" And when Rhue still didn't answer, "Ah, man, you already called him, he knows you're here. You can't disappear again without talking to him."

"I'm, uh, ..."

"You are one sorry son of a—"

Wizard was tugging Rip's sleeve. "C'mon. He got us clear of the cops. He doesn't have to tell us nothing."

"Hell, he doesn't. I didn't have to go into that flaming warehouse either, but—"

"Rip, let's go. It's over."

When the city bus slid to a halt at the corner, they were both staring hard ahead, their backs lined up like pickets. The thrust of Rip's shoulders so stiff, he might as well not have known there was anyone else on the street.

Rhue took a step closer. The cast scraped the pavement. "My son doesn't know anything about me. How can I explain what I did, who I am? He'll never understand."

Snorting with disgust, Wizard took the bus steps two at a time, but Rip waited until the last possible minute, then sprinted through the doors. He called back as the rubber edges whipped together. "You've got it all wrong, old man, he doesn't need to understand you. You need to understand him."

The doors shut and the bus groaned into the traffic. Adrift on the empty sidewalk, Rhue watched the bus spurt in spits and starts until it turned the corner and disappeared.

All these years he had resisted overtures from Joey Clark's son and the other ranch hands. With barely disguised disdain he'd relegated them to non-entities, the imposed distance justified because they had no experience, because they hadn't traveled where he had. But like Rip and Wizard, the younger cowboys had simply danced to different music. The lost opportunities caught him in the middle like a sucker punch. For all Rip and Wizard knew, he actually was the derelict they'd found in a phone booth, self-centered and unreliable.

When the taxi stopped at the curb before he signaled, he was so surprised he climbed in. The driver asked three times for his destination before Rhue answered with the name of a hotel he'd passed on his trip to Penn Station yesterday. Two blocks from the precinct, he remembered the duffle bag and re-directed the taxi to the train station.

A different man stood guard at the baggage check. Although he surveyed Rhue's Stetson and the cast, the employees must have been talking about the traveling cowboy. "You're late. They approved the release last night, but there was no answer at the phone number you left."

Rhue was positive the man didn't want to know where he'd been overnight. He pointed to the cast. "Hard to get around."

Grunting, the fellow disappeared into the back and came back with the duffle over his shoulder. "This is what all the hoopla's about?"

Although Rhue was relieved when he finally had the bag in his hands, it made his quandary all the more real. The money had taken on a significance he didn't fully understand. Why had he brought it? Insurance against going back to Montana? If he failed with Ford, he could hardly offer him the money. *Here's something to remember your lousy father.* The money wouldn't serve as compensation. What an insult that would seem coming from a man who had stayed away so long.

From the hotel room he could see all the way down Broadway. There were no trees. No flamingo sunrise flamed at the horizon. No horizon at all, just a narrowing of the perspective until the buildings and pavement blurred into gray nothingness. The hotel window had been constructed so that it didn't open. Loud air conditioning machinery purified the city air until it smelled almost clinical inside the room. He missed the pungent smell of peat burning in the ranch house woodstove. He missed the deserted corral at dawn. He missed the horses.

Once he'd squared things with Ford, he'd go back. The decision, finally articulated, relieved him. Adriana's death made it easier. He didn't need Cecily to foretell his future to know that, unlike Marian, he couldn't accept the inevitability of growing feeble. He'd find another horse and ride into the hills he loved. In Montana there was no one to stop him from making a fool of himself. Halfway across the country Ford would feel no obligation to visit, no pressure to waste time taking care of an old man who was racing toward the next world.

If he did persuade Ford to keep the money, it might give his son a chance to break out of boundaries that were restrictive, to take advantage of an opportunity he wouldn't otherwise pursue. It would be vicarious living in a way. And if he refused, Rhue would see that the boys had it. Detective Long could find them. The money would give them options. In his mind it had always represented the time he'd spent with the horses. Tangible and concrete, it symbolized his own choice to pursue a dream. All those years of freedom weighed him down here, suddenly, faced with the consequences. So the money was an easy thing to give away. He wouldn't miss it.

He called Maurice on the hotel phone.

"I think they're headed back." Maurice confirmed without saying when they'd called.

"If it's not too much trouble, I'll need the key again in about an hour."

Maurice mumbled something and Rhue wondered, with the background noise, if the poor fellow had visitors or was still sitting in front of the television where he'd been that morning. Ambushed by the old disillusionment, the remembered feeling of disconnect, of moving through swarms of people without acknowledging any human bond, he felt sorry for Maurice, alone and keeping dogs for company. He felt sorry for Detective Long who had to assume the worst about everyone.

But he no longer felt sorry for himself. Although he was here begging for a relationship with a son who had every right to refuse, he felt more hopeful than most of the people who lived here in the city of lights. His son hadn't refused outright. He was coming back, maybe not eager to embrace a long-lost father, but at least willing to talk.

When Rhue closed his eyes and imagined his son winding down the interstate and crossing the cobalt Hudson into the noisy tangle of city streets, he smelled again the damp grass of the lion's cage, the sizzle of train wheels on metal track, and the invisible stirring of air under Delilah's nostrils. Despite all his failures, hope had sprung from something, something that had happened to him since the deserted train station in Montana.

Once the bellboy brought the requested masking tape to the room, Rhue strapped the plastic laundry bag from the closet over the cast and hurried through a shower. The water ran black where the warehouse smoke had filtered into his hair. His laughter gurgled with the water. Rip would have found it amusing too.

Afterward Rhue ate the room service meal he'd ordered before the shower, thinking how much more he'd enjoyed the cafeteria with the boys. He took the next bite before he finished the one before. Food was strength. The digital clock on the bedside dresser clicked at each minute's change. Time marched on like shadows of pedestrians at dusk, silent and distinguishable only in outline, gone before you recognized the shape. Click after click, it inched away from him as if it were anxious to slip away unnoticed. And he, very aware of its passage, paid much more careful attention, conserving all but the most necessary movements as if he too might wind down into an inert mass without character or energy.

The importance of being at the apartment when Ford arrived loomed more significant as time passed. Rhue unpacked just enough. He pulled clean clothes from the duffle and dressed in spare, deliberate movements. Before going down, he took care to apply four of the hotel's Band-aids to the blister under the cast.

"Did the front desk call ahead for your taxi, sir?" The bellman held the street door wide.

"No, I—" The breeze caught the rim of his hat and he had to grab at it to keep it from flying. As he felt himself falling, he lunged for the railing. Momentum swung him down and around so that he ended up on his hip with his good leg on top of the broken one. Guests behind him skirted his legs with hardly a pause and continued out to the sidewalk.

"Excuse me," the bellman stretched out the words in disgust. "Crazy people. In such a damn hurry they gotta step over a cripple man." He helped Rhue up and propped him next to the rail by the sidewalk, blocking the passage with his bulk. "You okay? We got a wheelchair right inside. Maybe you should sit for a minute, let everything settle back to the right place."

Shaking his head, Rhue laughed. Vince and Marian would roll at the idea of Rhue off-balance, relegated to a wheelchair. That perspective, the ability not to take himself so seriously, that's what they'd given him, that's what he missed. The city life he and Adriana had shared had been a whirlwind of social events. Most of the people they'd associated with were eager to show off the money they were making, not that they weren't generous to the causes they supported.

He longed for the simpler loyalty of the horses and his friends. But that world, those friends were gone. From this distance he was no longer sure it had been real. For the first time in a long time the future was uncertain. Yet, he wasn't at all sure he wanted things back the way they'd been. Even though he fit in that world and here he was awkward and unsure, not coming would have left a huge void. If Ford had found the same kind of satisfaction in his work and his friends, a relationship with his father would be a bonus, but not essential.

The uniformed man slapped the hood of the next taxi in the queue and the door lock popped up. Although a woman with a briefcase protested, the bellman glared and she stepped back. Steering Rhue past her, he helped him into the open back seat. "There you go."

When the taxi dropped him at Ford's building for the second time, he almost signaled the cabbie to wait. For that minute on the pavement he savored the slight tinge of rose beyond the buildings to the west. It hinted at what existed beyond the city, places he knew and some he didn't. There were still parts of the world he'd never explored, a tease he considered for the briefest moment. But loneliness was there too. A place, even one that fit your personality, that inspired your dreams, couldn't match a hand on your shoulder or a whisper at bedtime. It was finding the right balance that was so complicated.

In the constant motion of cars and pedestrians he tried to see beyond the crowded urban landscape into the future. There was a great blank space for where he was headed. Vince might be gone and Marian lost, but the time spent with them hadn't been wasted. Closeness brought real understanding and lent permanence beyond any single human life. If Ford would listen, if Rhue could make him listen, it might not be too late for his son.

When he'd left Adriana all those years ago, words had failed him. He didn't want that to happen again. He had minutes, maybe less, to fine tune what he'd say, to sort through the last forty years and find something to convince his son that dreaming by itself wasn't enough to sustain a person.

Maurice answered the first knock. "Ah, Rip Van Winkle. I was worried."

Rhue felt self-conscious as Maurice took in the change of clothes, the new scrape on his cheek, the battered Stetson.

Motioning Rhue into the foyer, Maurice held the door. "I just figured it out. You two never met before." He waited for Rhue's nod, then slapped his thigh, as if congratulating himself for getting it right. "Ford's always been laid back, but on the phone, talking about you, he was more nervous than a rookie pitcher on opening day. You don't know him, but he's not one of those Wall Street con artists. He's genuinely nice."

Rhue wasn't sure how to answer. "The key?"

"You won't need it." Maurice turned away, the conversation over.

The panic rose in Rhue's throat and he couldn't make the words sound in the chilly block of empty space.

"Wait. I need—" He was choking, struggling to put all the emotion of the last week into words that would convince Maurice not to leave him there by himself. At his doorway Maurice swung around. He looked confused at Rhue's still being there.

"Ford has the key. He's back. You can go up."

Maurice walked him to the elevator, but didn't comment on his silence. As Rhue rode the elevator this time, his throat was dry and his chest ached with anticipation. Here he was, minutes from seeing his son, taking his hand, hearing his voice. In spite of Rhue's nervousness, he felt again, for different reasons, that exhilaration at the sight of Delilah as she streaked across the open plain. Old as he was, the possibilities were as fresh and enticing as their evening waltz.

Somewhere out there Cecily was crooning old love songs to a new stranger. Keeping watch. And Rip and Wizard were struggling with schoolbooks and promises, each eager to make their own way. Even Joey Clark's boy was using words to entice one of Tiara's girls to go upstairs with him. It was an old story. It was a new story.

Rhue practiced the lines he'd been composing the last five days. The power of words, he'd had it all along, right from the beginning. He just hadn't known how important it was. In the hallway, his hand raised to Ford's door, he looked out the narrow window. One by one the city lights appeared. Some were close enough to feel their warmth and some so far he had to squint to be sure they were real. The stars on the prairie had been like that at first.

Acknowledgements

Cowboys hold a special place in the hearts of Americans and adventurers everywhere. The appealing simplicity and honesty, so central to a cowboy's way of life, fascinate us, especially when contrasted with their avoidance of the real world complications of family relationships. The idea of this particular cowboy waltzing with Delilah in the opening scene came to me years ago, most likely inspired by that first Marguerite Henry book and the countless riding lessons and horse shows, to which I dragged my mother. George Garrett, former UVA English Dept Chair and Virginia Poet Laureate, and Steve Boykewich, Editor of *Meridian Literary Journal,* awarded first place to that story in the annual *HooK* contest in 2004. Rhue's prairie dance with Delilah stood on its own as a story until his past in New York City rose up like a ghostly mourner from Vince's funeral and begged me to explore Ford's life as a son without a father. I have to thank my own father for my magical childhood and the lesson of responsibilities assumed. And my father-in-law for being there when I needed him.

Without my loyal and ruthless critique group, Bonnie, Susan and JeanAnne and my long distance writing friends Sylvia May and Barbara Shine, the manuscript might have languished. And without Gary Kessler, an enthusiastic editor with a cowboy's brutal honesty, I might not have found the impetus to push Rhue and Ford to their full potential. And again, I am forever grateful for the continuing support and encouragement of Cedar Creek Publishing and all those wonderful readers out there.

Discussion Points for Book Clubs

1. What character traits allowed Rhue to make a life for himself as a cowboy, a single person on the prairies? How do those same character traits impose difficulties on his desire to be forgiven by his son?

2. How do Ford's memories of his childhood inform his own self-image as a man and as a potential lover?

3. What defines a good parent?

4. If Rhue had stayed in New York, consider the likely outcome for Ford and for the Hogan family. Is any father/mother better than no father/mother?

5. Should a person who has abdicated responsibility for a child or a wife be allowed to come back and be involved in his family's life? Are there limits on what that person should be allowed to share?

6. Were there things that Adrianna could or should have done to persuade Rhue to stay?

7. How does Rhue's long-term commitment to the horses and to his friends change your perspective on his flight from the pregnant Adrianna?

8. What effect did Rhue's absence have on Ford's ability to fall in love or find a partner?

9. How important are the city boys to Rhue's decision to wait for Ford to come back? How about Melanie?

10. How do the parallels between father and son contribute to the reader's understanding of the challenges faced by parents who give up early on?

11. When is it that Ford finally realizes he can be a good partner for Evie? What does it have to do with his forgiveness of his own father, if at all?

12. Can a person be courageous and frightened at the same time? How does fear of failure affect one's ability to face a challenge or an enemy, whether it's an idea or a person?

13. What flaws, strengths or weaknesses, of the other characters change Rhue's vision of himself? Or Ford's vision of himself?

14. Is escape a remedy for fear?

BONUS SHORT STORY
by Sarah Collins Honenberger

Looking to Beat the Odds

*N*inety-five sizzling hot dollar bills newly won at the Blackjack table, gone with the wind. Monopoly money. A flutter, a dot, gone. Stan's brand new Miller Cattleman disappeared behind the convertible. He clutched at the air, eyes wide at the sudden emptiness, and then just laughed. If he didn't mind, I wasn't about to complain. His car, his gas, I was just along for the ride. But I didn't want to be careless about it either. I anchored my matching ten gallon on my lap.

With Stan behind the wheel and the glittering rattler of Interstate 15 stretched out ahead of us, I was enjoying the way the hot dry air off the Nevada desert plowed through my hair. It was how I imagined a wind tunnel would be. Not that I'd ever even seen a real wind tunnel, but it wasn't too hard to imagine how strong wind like that would drag your hair and skin backwards, making the bones in your face stand out, your lips dry. You'd look different, feel different, but you'd be the same.

Let me set the record straight. I'm not in the habit of accepting gifts from men, but there was something about Stan right from the beginning. By total chance I happened to be sitting next to him when he won a mother lode at *The Golden Nugget*. He kissed me— simply celebrating with the only female close enough—and I kissed him back. Simply bored.

Something happened in that three seconds. It wasn't the kiss exactly. Kisses are a dime a dozen in Vegas and I had enough to fill any slot machine bucket. For almost a year I'd been waiting tables and watching the gamblers. Dreaming about what could be, but not doing a damn thing about it. And hiding out from a guy back home, Lou, who wanted to get married and have fourteen children. Too nice, too boring. I'd learned that much about myself at least.

When Stan stepped back from the kiss to take a breath, he looked at me like a blind man who'd just been given sight. Unreal how it felt to have a stranger know you instantly and completely. And the peace, the feeling of my whole soul settling. No quivers of arousal, no shivers of anticipation. Or danger. Just peace.

Who would have guessed? Sitting on a stool watching strangers pick up little black and red rectangles and move piles of chips back and forth. Thinking about how sad it was that I didn't want Lou or his fourteen children when a hundred women would paint their nails blue to have that chance.

Stan offered to buy me dinner. After the kiss, it probably seemed like the logical way to go. The cowboy hats were in the window of the lobby gift shop on the way out. Once he'd bought the hats, he changed his mind about dinner and said he was due in Provo in the morning, did I want to ride along. I've never been there, I said. He just signaled a bellboy, gave him a twenty, and asked him to help me with my bags.

Halfway to the elevator I turned back. Stan hadn't moved. What I wanted to ask was how he'd known I lived here, worked here, that the casino wrote my paychecks. Lucky guess?

What I said was, "I'm Maureen, Renie for short."

"Stan," he said, "Stan Lathrop."

"You sure you want to take a chance on a girl you don't know?"

"The girls I know aren't worth betting on. Take your time. I'll wait."

The convertible was his idea too. When I came back down, he was in the circular drive outside the hotel lobby in a rented car, a nondescript sedan. Maybe it was all he could afford when he came into town, but it didn't look like the right fit at all. Especially with the hat. The bellboy put my two mismatched suitcases in the trunk next to a battered overnight bag and a bulging black duffle. When he patted the side panel twice like the rump of a horse, I hopped in. He grinned and waved. Maybe it was the matching hats or the fact that he knew Stan and I were strangers.

Instead of taking the highway north, Stan turned south on Boulevard and drove straight to the Cadillac dealership on East Sahara Avenue. He parked the sedan by the front door and walked in with two fistfuls of cash. They must be used to that in Vegas.

"Silver?" the dealer repeated. "Only one on the lot is cobalt blue. I could have a silver one by Friday."

"Cobalt blue?" Stan asked me.

"Blue's great. Smooth, confident."

"Cobalt blue it is," Stan said and started counting. He sent me back to the car for more, but it hardly made a dent on the pile in his duffle.

We crossed the state line in the pitch black. The desert offered up its own kind of deep and endless anonymity. The car, an oasis.

"What're you thinking?" Stan asked, his fingers on the radio knob, Mr. Polite turning down the volume like he actually cared what I thought.

I hesitated. I haven't had much practice with the truth, but Stan didn't deserve a lie.

"I guess you're hungry. I cheated you out of that steak dinner." Stan's fingers had abandoned the radio knob for my knee.

"I'm not hungry." I ran my fingers along the brim of the hat. Waterproof felt meant to last, but softer than my grandma's cheek. "I'm not thirsty. I don't know how to describe it. I've never felt quite like this before."

"Good or bad?"

"Don't know that yet."

"A woman of mystery." He'd found the torn place in my jeans and was worrying it gently.

"A woman of contradictions."

"Fair enough." He turned the radio back on, then his hand went back to the tear.

Stan drove. I slept, longer and harder than I'd slept since I disappeared on Lou. When I woke up, my head was on Stan's shoulder and he was singing with the radio. I could feel the thrumming in his chest. Different. Nice.

"A man of many talents." I propped my boots up on the door, feeling unused muscles stretching and pulling. His body felt solid behind me. I let my head fall back in place.

His fingers went back to the knob, that polite thing again. Funny though, how it was starting to feel real.

"I don't think I've sung anything for ten years," he said. "Maybe twenty. Hymns were the last thing I sang. The only thing. My uncle was a traveling preacher. I used to know the entire Baptist hymnal. Give me a first line and I could sing it."

"Am I supposed to believe that means you like hymns?"

He smiled back, instantaneous enough to be reminiscent of the bellboy. "You're a mind-reader now? Maybe we should go back to Vegas. You could read the cards and we'd double our money."

"Double or nothing?" I shook my head. "Let's just drive to Provo and see what happens."

We didn't make it to Provo. At a roadside saloon outside of Cedar City dinner turned into dancing. Dancing turned into kissing. Kissing turned into more kissing. It's an old story. But this time it was different. We walked back to the motel room, Stan's arm around my waist, my hand looped into his belt. He pointed out stars and listened to me about losing my only brother in a car accident without once interrupting. I'm not sure I've ever told anyone the whole story before.

They say that home is where the heart is. I've looked in a lot of places. I knew I didn't want to go back to Lou. And I didn't want fourteen kids. Vegas, with its lights and drama and glitz, had seemed the least boring of the places I'd tried. But it had never seemed like home.

You're thinking you know how this goes. Back at the motel room, two strangers after dancing and kissing and talking about the stars. But I warned you right from the beginning this was different. Stan had a chess set in his suitcase. A man who liked games, I should have guessed that. Maybe I should have been nervous.

He showed me all the ways the pieces could move and taught me how to set them up to start. He talked me through a practice game. Strategy, power, versatility. He took off his shoes and rubbed his feet against mine under the table. He never touched the TV.

"Okay, set 'em up again," he said. "If you beat me, you can have the duffle and the car. If you lose, you stay with me for the summer."

I tipped the cowboy hat back off my forehead so I could see his eyes. "What happened to winner take all?"

For more great stories and author news, visit:
www.readhonenberger.com